A CONVENIENT BRIDE FOR THE SOLDIER

Christine Merrill

MILLS & BOON

Published in Great Britain 2017
by Mills & Boon, an imprint of HarperCollins*Publishers*
1 London Bridge Street, London, SE1 9GF

© 2017 Harlequin Books S.A.

Special thanks and acknowledgement are given to Christine Merrill
for her contribution to The Society of Wicked Gentlemen series.

ISBN: 978-0-263-92602-6

Printed and bound in Spain
by CPI, Barcelona

Christine Merrill lives on a farm in Wisconsin, USA, with her husband, two sons, and too many pets—all of whom would like her to get off of the computer so they can check their e-mail. She has worked by turns in theatre costuming and as a librarian. Writing historical romance combines her love of good stories and fancy dress with her ability to stare out of the window and make stuff up.

Books by Christine Merrill

Mills & Boon Historical Romance

The de Bryun Sisters

The Truth About Lady Felkirk
A Ring from a Marquess

Ladies in Disgrace

Lady Folbroke's Delicious Deception
Lady Drusilla's Road to Ruin
Lady Priscilla's Shameful Secret

The Society of Wicked Gentlemen

A Convenient Bride for the Soldier

Stand-Alone Novels

A Wicked Liaison
Miss Winthorpe's Elopement
Dangerous Lord, Innocent Governess
Two Wrongs Make a Marriage
Unlaced at Christmas
'The Christmas Duchess'
The Secrets of Wiscombe Chase
The Wedding Game

Mills & Boon Historical *Undone!* eBooks

Seducing a Stranger
Virgin Unwrapped
To Undo a Lady

Visit the Author Profile page
at millsandboon.co.uk for more titles.

To the boys in the basement.
Not Stephen King's boys. Mine.
Here's to getting the band back together.

Chapter One

The dancers stopped and the musicians set down their instruments. Georgiana Knight had never been so glad to hear a song end.

'You dance like an angel.' Her partner, Sir Nash Bowles, showed no sign of releasing the hand he was holding, instead attempting to tuck it into the crook of his arm so he could escort her from the dance floor.

Had she heard the compliment, her stepmother would have been quick to point out that George was as far from angelic as it was possible for a girl to be. In Marietta's opinion, George was lacking in both good sense *and* manners. In the years after her mother's death, her father had allowed her to run wild in the country like a hoyden. The resulting damage to her character was most likely irreparable.

Which was just fine with George. She was happy, just as she was. She certainly did not want to be anyone's angel. It made her think of dancing on a pinpoint, instead of the razor's edge of courtesy on which she was balanced when dealing with Sir Nash. He was Marietta's cousin. Any rudeness on her part would be reported back to her stepmother, which would result in another tiresome lecture on deportment during the carriage ride home.

She yanked her hand free of his grasp with such suddenness that she almost left him holding an empty glove. Sir Nash was sure to tattle about it and there would be another row.

Perhaps it was not too late to mitigate the damage. George gave him the sweetest smile she could manage, but made no effort to take his arm. 'Thank you, sir. You are an excellent dancer as well.' It was one of the many virtues, along with wealth and family connection, that Marietta would throw in her face when George refused his inevitable offer.

Sir Nash reached for her hand again, as though he had more right to touch her than she had to refuse. 'Another dance, perhaps? I hear the orchestra leader tuning up for a waltz.'

She had to fight the shudder that rose at

the prospect. He had managed to stand far too close to her in the most ordinary of line dances. Lord knew what he might attempt if given an excuse to hold her in his arms. 'I would not want to stand up, only to stop before the dance was over.' She reached for her fan and snapped it open, creating a fragile barrier between them. Then she closed it and touched it to her left ear, using the language of signals that ladies had created to avoid embarrassing scenes.

I want you to leave me alone.

Then she finished with words that they should both know were nothing more than a polite lie to save him embarrassment. 'The last set left me quite fatigued. I think it best to sit for a while.'

'I will find us chairs,' he said, ignoring her hint, her tone, and everything else she had done in the last weeks to dissuade him from pursuing her. There was a faint sibilance when he spoke that always reminded her of the hiss of a snake. Though his body was far too stocky too support the serpentine analogy, his movements, whether dancing or walking, were smooth and silent. Even when she was not with him, she feared that he might appear suddenly to offer an inappropriate word or an unwelcome touch.

Now she laid the fan against her left cheek. *No!*

'It is not necessary to escort me,' she said to reinforce the signal, snapping the fan open and giving it a furious flutter. 'I must attend to necessities.' It would have been so much easier had he been the sort of fellow who trod on hems. Short of ripping her gown herself she had no excuse to give other than a call of nature, to hide in the lady's retiring room. Let him think what he wished about her reasons for going there, as long as she did not have to say aloud that she was trying to escape from him.

He gave a nod of defeat and let her go. But she knew, by the creeping feeling of the hairs at the back of her neck, that he watched each retreating step to make sure of her destination.

Once safely behind the door, she dropped into the nearest chair, ignoring the bustle of the ladies around her. Why was it that the most unappealing men were always the most persistent? The fact that Sir Nash was from her stepmother's family made it all the more awkward. Marietta was continually singing the man's praises in hopes of a match that, if George had any say in it, would never occur.

She shuddered again. As much as she did not like Marietta, she must make some effort to maintain peace for Father's sake. But that did not mean she had to dance more than a courtesy set with Sir Nash.

'Georgiana!' Her stepmother's voice cut through her introspection like a shard of glass.

'Yes, Marietta,' she said with a sigh.

'Sir Nash says you are unwell.'

'And you came to see if it was true,' George finished for her.

'I do not want you malingering in the retiring room when you should be enjoying yourself.'

'I am enjoying myself,' George replied, unable to contain the truth. 'I find it much more enjoyable to be here, alone, than dancing with your cousin.'

'Horrible, wilful girl.' Her stepmother was looking at her with the usual, thinly disguised loathing. The woman liked her no better at nineteen than she had seven years ago, when she had married Father. George had long ago given up trying to gain an approval that would never come.

Now she resisted the urge to pull a face and

behave like the spoiled child Marietta proclaimed her to be. 'I am trying to be polite. If
I have no interest in his suit, it would be cruel
of me to give him false hope.'

'If you think rejecting him without reason
is a virtue, you are sorely mistaken,' Marietta
snapped.

'I have reason enough,' she said, glancing
around. Their argument was drawing enough
attention without her elaborating on the sordid
details of her time with Sir Nash.

'If I thought that your desire to hang on your
father's coat-tails was a reason to avoid marriage, then I would agree with you.'

'Were it true, it would be no different than
marrying me off to your cousin, so you can get
me out of your house,' George said sharply. 'I
am more than willing to go. But not if I must
marry Nash Bowles.' Now her face contorted
in the grimace she had been trying to contain. But she could not help it. At the mention
of the man's name, all that was in her recoiled
in revulsion.

'Georgiana!'

It was the beginning of what was likely to
be a colourful harangue about her deficient
character, made all the more humiliating by

the dozen or so women and maids who were pretending that they were not listening to every word. She would not stand for it. She would go and sit in the carriage if she had to. Perhaps, if she begged, the driver would take her back to the country where she belonged, for she'd had not a moment's peace since the day they'd arrived in London. George shot up and out of her chair, pushing past Marietta and through the door, slamming it behind her.

She had not thought it possible for the evening to get worse. But on the other side, she all but ran into the only person she wanted to see less than Sir Nash.

Mr Frederick Challenger was lounging against the wall just opposite the door. What reason did he have to lurk outside the ladies' room? Or was he possessed of some evil instinct that drew him to be where she was, so he might prevent her from regaining even a little of her pride?

Now he behaved as he did whenever he saw her. He did not bother with the sort of polite acknowledgement she would have got even from a rotter like Sir Nash. Instead, he glanced in her direction with a half-smile and then looked through her, as if she didn't exist.

It was just as he'd done since the first moment they'd met. If one could call a glimpse that had not ended in an introduction a meeting. It had been at Almack's, some weeks past. Marietta had been all but dragging her by the ear towards him. 'You must meet Mr Challenger, Georgiana. He is the second son of the Earl of Roston, a hero of Waterloo, eligible and rich!' She had said it loud enough for all in the vicinity to hear.

At least, it had been loud enough for Mr Challenger to hear and be insulted. He had cast a blank look in their direction, then turned and walked away before they could speak to him. And so it had gone at each meeting since. Apology was impossible, since they had not been introduced. Not that she should have to be sorry for a thing that was none of her doing. In fact, if he were a gentleman, he should have pretended not to have heard words that were clearly not meant for his ears.

But it seemed that his chief talent was sticking his perfect nose where it did not belong. Wherever she went, he was there, always watching her while pretending not to notice, never speaking, but always smiling as she made one faux pas after another. Why should she be surprised that he'd caught her red-faced and angry, fresh from the latest argument?

For a moment, their eyes met, accidentally, she was sure. His were already sliding away to make her painfully aware of his disinterest. In response, she directed all the petty irritations of the night at him in a wordless cry that was part anger and part exasperation.

He awarded her with a slightly raised eyebrow, as if to say he was aware of her presence, but thoroughly glad he did not have to speak to her.

She took a deep breath to regain control and answered with what she'd hoped was a dignified sniff that would declare him rude and beneath her notice. Then she swept past him, towards the outer doors.

That was the moment she discovered her skirt had caught in the slammed door behind her. Her grand exit was marred by the sound of ripping gauze and a confetti shower of spangles on the rug at her feet. Since the retiring room was one of the many places she'd been trying to escape, there was no point in going back for a repair. Instead, she grabbed what was left of her skirt and ran for the door, followed by the faint sounds of a man's chuckle.

* * *

'…and then she ran through the ballroom, with her petticoat exposed, almost to the waist.'

'It was an accident,' George muttered for what seemed like the hundredth time. She sat in the carriage seat opposite her stepmother, elbow on the windowsill and her chin resting on her fist, gazing outside at the London traffic.

'Peace, Marietta.' Her father's voice drifted from where he sat beside his wife, staring out of his own window. 'She did not mean to do it.' Then he sighed.

Even as he defended her he sounded faintly disappointed. He had loved her once, George was sure. But lately, when he spoke, he always sounded tired. Was it of London and the demands of Parliament? Or was he simply tired of her?

'Georgiana has far too many such accidents,' Marietta proclaimed. 'Since you did not bother to teach her manners, someone must. It amazes me that she has attracted any interest at all on the marriage mart.'

'Which brings us back to Sir Nash, just as I knew it would,' George said, grimacing again. 'Marry me off if you mean to, but find someone else. I will not have him.'

Her stepmother drew herself up in indignation. 'There is nothing wrong with Sir Nash. He is an honoured member of my family.'

'I do not doubt it. But that does not mean I have been able to manufacture a romantic attachment to him where none exists.'

'But, unlike the rest of London, he is quite taken with you,' Marietta said.

So now all of London hated her. If Mr Challenger was any indication, perhaps they did.

Marietta continued. 'In fact, he has assured me that there is no other girl in England who would make him happy.'

'And there is no man in the world who would make me less so.' She turned to her father for support. Even if he did want her gone, he had met Sir Nash. He must understand how hopeless this plan was.

'You have said similar things about all the other men Marietta has recommended,' her father said with another sigh, not looking back from the window.

'Because all the men Marietta has recommended are wrong for me.' She blurted the words before she could stop herself, immediately frustrated by her own lack of diplomacy.

But it was true. She had done no better when looking for herself. It felt as if she had danced with every man in town and not a one of them had interested her.

Marietta nudged her father with a fingertip to demand his attention and gave a knowing nod as if to say that this was proof that George was just as difficult as they both thought.

Now Father turned to her with the distant look he wore so often lately. 'I am thoroughly tired of acting as arbiter in these domestic squabbles.'

George smiled with relief. It was the arguments that bothered him and not her, after all. How shocked Marietta would be at the set down that was about to come. While Father might have some affection for his second wife, it was nothing compared to what he had always shown to his only child.

Then, he spoke. 'You must marry, Georgiana. You are nineteen and no longer a child. I see no reason that it cannot be to Sir Nash.'

'But...' She did not know how to go on. It had never occurred to her that, when the moment finally came that he was forced to decide the issue, her father would take Marietta's side against her.

'He dined with us just last night and seemed genuinely fond of you.'

'He…' She shook her head, unsure of how to explain what had been wrong with the evening. The man had said nothing untoward when they'd spoken last night, or on any other. He had been almost too polite. But then, as he had sat beside her on the sofa, he had mentioned a liking for snuff and offered her a pinch from his box.

She had found it unusual, but faintly intriguing. It must be pleasant, or people would not take it. But since she could think of no proper woman who used it, there must be something scandalous about it. In the end, she had refused, not sure that even her normally lenient father would approve.

Sir Nash had given an indifferent shrug and set the box on the table near the fire in case she changed her mind. It had been a somewhat bizarre flirtation, but not harmful. Then, she had looked at the box again.

At first glance, the scene painted on the top of the smooth stone box was just as ordinary as the evening. A young couple in a woodland glade: he entreating, and she shielding her face with her hand and refusing with a shy smile.

But then, Sir Nash had taken another pinch and set the box down again, tapping the lid and drawing her gaze to it. The picture had changed. The girl, who had been wearing a pink gown, did not seem to be wearing anything at all. The hand to her face looked less like an innocent refusal and more like a desperate, frightened denial.

The boy who had been with her was no longer a boy at all. His chest was bare and his legs were hair-covered and ended in the cloven hooves of a goat. But the place where those legs met was as human as a Greek statue. And he was doing…

Something.

George was not exactly sure what was going on. But the girl in the miniature looked both revolted and compelled. By the strange way George felt when she looked at it, she was sure that it was something she was not supposed to know about. And the snuffbox was something that no decent gentleman would show to a young lady he was courting.

When he was sure she had seen it, Sir Nash picked up the box and dropped it into his pocket again. Then he gave her a knowing smile and remarked at how pretty her hair was and how much he favoured blondes.

Blondes like the one on the snuffbox.

'You see?' When she came back to herself, Marietta was pointing again. 'She cannot come up with a logical reason for this refusal.'

'I do not like him,' George said, more weakly than before.

Because he showed me something I do not understand and I am afraid to ask you what it means.

'Affection sometimes grows with time.' Her father sounded almost hopeful as he said it and cast a brief, disappointed glance to his wife before looking out the window again.

'I will not marry him. You cannot make me.' George almost shouted the words, trying to regain his attention.

'On the contrary, my dear. We can and you will.' Marietta favoured her with a cool glare. 'Either you marry Nash, or I will go.' Then she turned to her husband and gave him the tight, uncompromising quirk of her lips that she thought was a smile. 'I can no longer bear things as they are. Surely you must see that. Either you bring your daughter to heel, or I will go back to the Continent where I am sure to find someone who will respect me. It will be the two of you, alone again, just as she wants.'

After seven years of strife, that sounded almost too good to be true. George turned to her father with hope in her eyes, and waited for his response.

When it came, it was not the vindication she sought, but another tired sigh. 'You have heard your mother, Georgiana. She is quite out of patience with you. Now let us have no more nonsense about refusing offers before they have been given, especially when they come from your mother's cousin.'

For a moment, she could not believe what she was hearing. He had been forced to choose. And without a moment's hesitation he had chosen Marietta. 'She is not my mother.' The words sounded childish, but she could not help them.

The carriage was just pulling up to the front of the Knight town house and she opened the door and jumped out before it had even fully stopped. Then she ran through the front doors, up the stairs, and to her room before her heart could break any further.

Inside, her maid was dozing in a chair, awaiting her arrival. She took one look at the ruined ballgown and murmured, 'Oh, miss', before reaching to help her out of it. 'Let me call for a cup of warm milk. Then we will put you to bed.'

'Do not treat me like a child,' George said, immediately regretting her temper. She took a deep, calming breath. 'I am sorry, Polly. But I do not want to go to bed. I do not want to spend another night in this house. Call for the trunks. We are going away.'

The girl looked up at her with a worried smile. 'Where are we going, miss?'

It was an excellent question and one for which she had no answer. There was not a relation near or distant who would keep her, if her father wanted her to come home. And she had never thought to put aside even a small portion of the generous allowance she'd been given against disaster. Until this moment, she'd never had an inkling that she might need to.

She sat down on the end of the bed. 'Never mind. I cannot think of a place we might go to.' She thought for a moment. 'And if I become a governess, I doubt my employers would allow me a lady's maid.'

'A governess, miss?' Polly gave her a knowing grin. 'Are you thinking about running away, again?'

Again. Had she really done it so often? It had become an idle threat she made, after particularly bad arguments with her stepmother. But the idea of employment had never lingered for more than a minute or two. She'd been an indifferent student. What good would she be as a teacher?

'I must do something,' she said, more to herself than the maid. 'I cannot marry Sir Nash.'

'Nash Bowles?' At the mention of marriage, her maid dropped any hint of formality. 'I will send for the trunks, immediately. We will get you away from here, so he cannot find you.'

'You know him?' She had not spoken of him in front of Polly. She had not even wanted to think about the man.

'All the servants know him. And the girls know to keep away from him.' The words ended in a whisper.

'Why?' But she suspected she did not want to know the answer.

'He…' Polly shook her head and left the sentence unfinished, just as George had done earlier. 'He is not a fit husband for a gently bred young lady. My brother says…' She paused again. 'Do you remember my brother Ben? He was a footman here until he outgrew all the livery.'

'I remember Ben.' Georgiana covered her mouth, trying to hide her smile. Ben Snyder had not just outgrown the uniform—he had far outstripped the other boys in size and weight. At six foot four, and seventeen stone, he'd towered over the rest of the staff and dashed Marietta's hopes for servants as evenly matched as the horses on the family carriage.

'When he left here, he went to work at a gentlemen's club. And the things that happen there...' Polly paused again. 'Well, he says that they are not the least bit gentlemanly. Even so, he has had to turf Nash Bowles out on more than one occasion for behaviour that the owners would not sanction.'

'So, he is not a gentleman?'

'He is not even a rake,' her maid confirmed. 'He is worse than that.'

It was just as she'd feared. The whole house seemed set on her marrying a lecher. 'What sorts of things does he do?'

'Ben would not tell me.'

'Would he tell Father?' And would the word of a former servant be enough to save her?

'I do not think he would do that, miss,' Polly

said. 'If Ben tells anyone what happens in the club, he risks losing his position. It is supposed to be very secret.'

'Perhaps, if there were a way to get Nash to admit to everything... Or, if I were to see it for myself...'

Polly's eyes grew round and she gave a warning shake of her head.

George smiled back with the first optimism she'd felt in ages. 'That is what I must do. If there are scandalous goings-on, there must be ladies in this club, mustn't there?'

'Not ladies, precisely,' said Polly.

'Cyprians!' *Even better.* 'Perhaps one of them will help me. And Ben will be there to protect me once I have discovered what Sir Nash wants from me. If the owners do not want things to be too scandalous, then I am sure they would rather have me escorted from the place than allow me to come to harm.'

'But if you are caught, the scandal will be real,' Polly reminded her.

'At least if I am ruined, no one will expect me to marry Sir Nash,' George said, with renewed confidence. If worse came to worst, she would take the veil and spend her remaining days in repentance. A life of celibacy and prayer was not something she wished for, but it would be free of the interference from Marietta and her detestable cousin.

'Come, Polly. We must write to your brother. And then you must help me to look like a fallen woman.'

Chapter Two

Forty members in attendance. Five-and-twenty guests of members. Staff above stairs: fifteen. Staff below stairs: ten.

Frederick Challenger walked through the ballroom of Vitium et Virtus, oblivious to the tumult around him, his mind still focused on the headcount he had taken passing through the rooms.

He could no longer remember what private joke had inspired the name Vice and Virtue when he and his friends had formed the club back at Oxford. There had always been plenty of the former, but he could remember not a single instance of the latter. And that utter lack of morality had turned the place from a college prank into the most decadent and most popular club in London.

It was that same popularity that made organised debauchery into a chore, and Frederick into the saner head that must prevail over the anarchy. Thus far, the night had been uneventful. In the game room, Lord Pendleton had attempted to continue play with an IOU after running though the money in his purse. It had taken only a gentle reminder from Fred that such a thing would render the masks that they all wore a moot point. One could not remain anonymous while announcing one's own identity with a signed marker. Of course, with his high voice and penchant for elaborate waistcoats, only an idiot would not know that Pendleton was there.

The real reason for cash play was much more simple. Watching a man continue to gamble until he had reduced himself to ruin spoiled the fun for everyone. And if someone blew his brains out at the table, it would make a hell of a mess. Fred had no desire to call upon Mrs Parker, the housekeeper, to arrange for the cleaning of the extremely expensive wallpaper, which was hand-painted silk that matched the Italian mural of a bacchanal on the ceiling.

In the main room, one of the club's infamous masked balls was in full sway. At the very centre of the dancers was some damned fool,

dressed as the devil. Rather than shrink from
the appearance of Old Scratch, the masked
dancers that thronged the dance floor raised
their hands in salute.

Fred had donned a domino mask and cape
for the sake of what passed as propriety. On
such nights, appearing without a costume drew
far more attention than red satin, horns and a
tail. As he pushed past him on the way to the
owners' private quarters, Lucifer gave a menacing wave of the cat-o'-nine-tails he held, as
if ready to strike.

Fred stared him down with a dark glance
worthy of any of the fiends of hell and the man
turned away and brought the silken cords of his
flail down on the bare shoulders of the nearest
dancing girl, instead.

She responded with a shudder of pleasure
and turned to Fred with outstretched arms and
mouth open for a kiss.

Fred obliged, but only briefly. Then he un-
tangled himself from her grip and thrust her
into the waiting embrace of a man on his left.
She offered a pout as brief as his kiss had been
before turning her attentions to her new partner.

'Me, next.' A buxom blonde dressed as a

randy milkmaid reached for him, tipping her head up and offering her lips.

He hid a sigh of frustration, forced a laugh and offered another kiss before breaking away to push past towards the green baize door that hid the corridor to the office.

It did not do for an owner of the club to be so unenthusiastic when tempted with sins of the flesh. When he and his friends had founded the secret society at Oxford, they had meant to give in to every temptation and take no vice in moderation. But what had seemed daring ten years ago felt rather silly now that all of London wanted to join them in their debauchery.

His friend, Oliver Gregory, thought that Fred's time in the army had sucked all the joy from his soul and rendered him the sort of authoritarian that they'd been rebelling against. That was hardly the case. He had his reasons to forgo the excesses here and had discovered he much preferred the military to hedonism. No matter how chaotic it had seemed, war had a brutal structure to it. Orders were given and received. Men knew their place and their reason for living and dying. On the battlefield, life had purpose. After Waterloo, Vitium et Virtus seemed the epitome of pointlessness.

The club's third owner, Jacob Huntington, had insisted that Fred was merely jaded. That if he could find some fresh, untried iniquity it would whet his appetite for life.

What a disappointment it must be that neither women nor gaming, or any overindulgence Fred could imagine, was as satisfying as knowing that when he was there to watch over it, the club ran like a well-oiled machine. Jake saw to it that the membership was limited to only the most sought-after dilettantes. After they had joined, Oliver made sure that the entertainments were every bit as excessive as they could have hoped. The food and drink had no equal in London. The games had the highest stakes.

Once the stage had been set for debauchery, the owners' jobs were almost ended. One did not need to order people to do that which they wanted in the first place. But Fred was the one to make sure everyone who passed the threshold stayed within the bounds of reasonable behaviour. When they left, he saw to it that they kept their mouths shut about what occurred and whom they had seen. There were no fist fights, no embarrassing scenes, and no females shrieking down the main stairs that they were being forced against their will. The women found at Vitium et Virtus, whether members or employees, were all ready and willing to sin.

If there was scandal, he dealt with it, quickly, quietly, and with as little drama as was possible. Before he had returned from Waterloo and taken over the day-to-day running of the place, they had given little thought to security. It had been naïve of them to believe that a den of libertines had no need of structure. That carelessness had reduced the initial number of owners from four to three. Friends were precious. He would not lose another.

Tonight, after his cursory examination of the revels, Fred meant to lock himself in the office with a glass of brandy and a good book. If they caught him at it, Oliver and Jake would be appalled and declare that some portion of him must have died on the battlefield to leave him so indifferent to the activities around him.

Perhaps they were right. He glanced at the laughing people surrounding him, utterly unmoved. Should a place of such unfettered pleasure be so bone-numbingly boring?

But as he passed by the last doorway before the office, the low rumble of the crowd piqued his deadened curiosity. This was the space set aside for the auctioning of favours.

There, masked courtesans might throw over their usual protectors for an evening and go away with whatever gentleman had the most money to offer them. If they decided to drop their disguise and reveal their beautiful faces, it was only after the bedroom door was closed.

It was a titillating thrill for all involved. One might find oneself sampling the favourite of the most powerful men in England. Or discover that one's own mistress, or worse yet, one's own wife, had grown so bored she'd decided to offer herself to any man willing to indulge her vanity.

Tonight, there was something about the fevered sound of the bidding that seemed *wrong*. Once Fred pushed past the crowd by the door it took only a glance to see that this was no ordinary auction. In front of him, the auctioneer shouted, 'How much, gentlemen, for a maiden-head? Turn out your pockets. Dig deep into your purses. Surely this beauty is worth more than the paltry bids I've heard.'

She stood on the small stage at the far end of the room as if floating on the cloud of tobacco smoke that hung over the men gathered at her feet. But the greasy light shining through the haze seemed to purify to an opalescent glow as it touched her skin.

And there was so much skin. Desire flooded him, sudden and unusual. She was beautiful and he wanted her. But another part of him wanted to rush forward and throw a coat over those bare shoulders to shield her from the roving eyes of the crowd. It was a sacrilege to look upon such untouched perfection. And she was an innocent. He was sure. Whores sometimes pretended to be virgins in these little games, hiding sponges of blood between their legs to fool their clients into believing they'd bought a deflowering. But they could not hide the look in the jaded eyes behind their masks, the knowing smile, or the lack of blush in their unrouged cheeks.

This girl was different. The downward cast of her masked head was not some ironic parody of shyness—it was genuine discomfort at being scrutinised. Her body was devoid of blemish except for the glow of embarrassment at her nakedness and the attention it had garnered.

Not quite naked, but near enough. She had not bothered with stays, chemise or stockings under the gown she wore, which was of a muslin so fine that it might as well have been a cloud of mist. When she moved, in the slow, awkward dance of one unaccustomed to seduction, the curtain of blonde hair that shielded her body parted revealing first a curve, then a dimple, and occasionally a glimpse of rose-tipped breasts, the hollow of her navel, or the delta of blonde curls between her legs.

As if that was not enough to make a man's breeches tight, the gold cord that tied her garments into a semblance of a classic tunic had been braided into a chain. The end of it wound around her throat and loosely bound each wrist. It incited fantasies of a captive slave at auction, unable to refuse any depravity a man could imagine for her.

Like the other frenzied bidders in the room, some dark corner of his soul was stirring. Had he ever lain with a virgin? If so, she had not been as sweet and untried as this one. The girl before him could not possibly know the fate that awaited her or the depths that a man might sink to when given the chance to indulge his most forbidden whims. One had only to look at Nash Bowles's reaction to see what was about to occur. That disgusting toad was every bit as recognisable as Pendleton had been, and the wad of banknotes he waved was easily the largest in the room. He was all but salivating as he shouted his bids.

Of course he would be here. Nash had often expressed his taste for untried blondes, the younger the better. Frederick had told him on more than one occasion that this was a club for mutual pleasure, not a dockside brothel. Then he'd made Snyder, the porter, escort him out the door. Tonight, Snyder stood behind the girl on stage, arms crossed on his chest, doing nothing to prevent what was going on.

It was all too much. The fact that Fred encouraged high stakes at the table and turned a blind eye to Dionysian revels did not mean that he had become a procurer for deviants. If he allowed this auction to continue, that would be exactly what he was. Without another thought, he grabbed for his purse and turned out the contents.

Not enough. So he stripped the gold ring from the finger on his hand and held it in the air. 'Ten thousand pounds!'

At this, a hush fell over the crowd and the auctioneer turned to him.

Disgusted, he tossed the ring towards the stage where it landed at the man's feet. 'It is

easily worth that. I have more. Should you refuse it, I will back it with a cheque for twice,
or thrice that amount.'

'No fair,' cried someone from the crowd.

'Foul,' cried another, to an increase of grum-
bling. 'You think that since you run this club
you can do what you like in it?'

Frederick grabbed the cat-o'-nine-tails from
the comic-opera Satan who had followed him
into the room and waved it menacingly over
his head. It was little more than a toy, but
combined with the ferocity of his tone, it was
enough to send the men around him scurrying
for the corners. 'Do I think I can do as I like?
Since I am the one to set the rules, I think I
can. I will have the lot of you chucked out into
the street and banned if you doubt me.'

He smiled, relishing the same surge of
power he got while frightening soldiers into
obedience in Portugal. 'But that will not be
all, you sad bunch of reprobates. Do you wish
your fathers, your wives, and your daughters to
know what a pack of disgusting, drunken lechers you are? If this room is not empty by the
time I count three, I will turn the club books
over to the tattle sheets. If you force my hand,
all of London will see how its finest sons be-

have when the sun is down and the curtains are drawn.' He laughed, bitter at the ridiculousness of it, and pointed to the door.

It was not even necessary to begin the count. All it took was a threat of exposure to send the crowd scurrying like rats. The stampede flowed around him, out the door. At the rear of the throng was the scantily clad virgin.

His arm came down to prevent her egress. 'And where do you think you are going?'

'You said…'

'I said they should leave. You have no permission to do so. You came here to sell yourself to the highest bidder. Now you are mine, bought and paid for. You will not leave from this place until I am done with you.' He grabbed the swaying tail of gold cord that dangled between her perfect breasts and led her back into the room.

She had come searching for a demon. Instead, she had found the devil himself.

Someone in the crowd had called him an owner. It would explain why Ben had vanished along with the rest of the men. Clearly, he was more afraid of losing his position than what might happen to her if she was caught here.

'No.' She tugged back against the tightening cord, stripping it from her wrists and throat. This was not as it was to have gone at all. Her plan had been working. Though he had worn a cape and mask, it had been obvious that Sir Nash had been the high bidder. His lisping voice was unmistakable. And then, this stranger had appeared and ruined everything.

It had been foolish of her to assume that anyone would protect her, should the plan go awry. Despite his promises, her supposed protector had not prevented a sale to someone else. Instead, Ben had given her a helpless shrug, recorded the transaction, and allowed the devil his due.

'No?' Beneath the half mask he wore, the club owner gave her a smile that was more of a leer. 'What makes you think you can refuse? Surely you knew what sort of club Vitium et Virtus was when you joined us.'

'Is that where I am?' There had been no name on the black-lacquered entrance door. Nor had she expected there to be rules in a place that was so clearly lawless.

'You are not a member, then.' He folded his arms across his impressively broad chest. Though there appeared to be a masquerade in progress, he was not wearing fancy dress. But neither had he bothered with formality. He wore no coat, waistcoat or cravat. His shirt was open, displaying fine muscles and a smattering of hair.

She snapped her eyes upwards, away from the bare skin directly in front of her. She had never seen so much of a man's body before, but she did not want this stranger to take her interest as something more than academic curiosity. 'If I am violating your by-laws by coming here, you had best turn me out immediately, as you threatened to do with the others.'

'When I am ready, not before.' There was something in his tone that implied her release would be a long time coming.

The prospect was terrifying. But something else as well. Perhaps it was the musk of sin in the air that was going to her head, but the fear she should be feeling was supplanted by an emotion that was unidentifiable and vaguely pleasant. He was tugging on her belt again, pulling her farther into the room. 'Where are you taking me?' She struggled for a moment, before realising that the flimsy belt was the only thing separating her from the loss of her gown.

'Into the light, where I can get a decent look

at you.' Then he laughed. 'Not that there is much I haven't seen, pretty one. Your dress is all but transparent.'

She'd thought it scandalous when she'd admired herself in her bedroom mirror. But if the plan had worked, she'd have been wrapped in a cloak and on her way home by now and not under the prurient scrutiny of this stranger. 'A gentleman would not have looked.'

He laughed again, his gaze travelling over her body like a lover's caress. 'When did I claim that I was a gentleman? And why do you object to my wanting a closer look at what I purchased? If you had been bought by any other man in this room, you would have more to fear than admiration. Did you think your ravisher would close his eyes as he took you? Or were you expecting a magical rescue from some man who paid good money to do whatever he liked with you?'

He said it with such obvious scorn that she did not want to admit her plan had been something very close to that. Although the man standing before her had made no move to assault her, she doubted she would escape the evening with her reputation intact. Even if he turned her out without further questioning, she might be forced to find her way home without help. The thought of knocking on her own front door in the flimsy costume she was wearing made her feel even more naked than she had before. She gave a hurried tug on the neckline of her gown, trying to regain some scrap of modesty, only to feel it rip in her hands to reveal even more of her body.

'Hell's teeth,' he muttered. For a moment, the air of menace he'd been projecting failed him and he seemed almost as confused as she felt by their current circumstances. He pulled the mask from his face and patted at his chest as if searching for a handkerchief in the coat he was not wearing that might wipe the nervous sweat from his brow.

'You!' Who else could it have been? The man had an unerring ability to appear, as if by magic, any time she did something remotely improper. But at least Frederick Challenger had been willing to snub her when he'd seen her in public. Now that they were alone, he could not seem to take his eyes of her. She ripped the mask from her own face. 'The least you could do is look me in the eyes, Mr Challenger.'

'Miss…Knight?' Did the hesitation in his

words mean that he was shocked by her presence here? Or had he actually forgotten her name?

'You admit you know me, then,' she said, triumphant. 'How unlike your behaviour at the ball the other night, where you looked right through me as though I did not exist.'

His leer had become a sarcastic smile. 'Does it really bother you so much when someone does not acknowledge you? Are you one of those young ladies so taken with your own allure that you cannot imagine a man capable of resisting you? Did you come here tonight just to gain my attention?'

How quickly his tune had changed, now that he knew her identity. When the masks were on, he had shown no signs of resisting her. In fact, she had been worried that the handsome stranger would insist that she follow through on the terms of the auction and that she might have no choice but to submit to some notorious rake.

The truth was both disappointing and annoying. 'I do not give a fig, Mr Challenger, whether men are caught by my allure, nor did I come here to teach you some sort of lesson. The fact that you would suggest such a thing tells me all I need to know about you. You are obsessed with your own importance.'

'As are you by demanding my attention,' he countered.

'It is a different thing entirely,' she argued. 'A lack of interest in another person does not normally translate into public rudeness. You make time to speak to every other lady in the room. But when I sought to be introduced, you walked away without a word.'

'Because I do not wish to encourage your behaviour, Miss Knight.'

'*My* behaviour?'

'Every time I see you, you are doing something outside the bounds of propriety. Dancing too close to your partners...'

'Not by choice,' she said, thinking of Sir Nash.

'Arguing with your mother...'

'She is my stepmother,' George interjected.

'It does not signify. Wearing indecent clothing...'

'The hem was caught in a door,' she finished for him.

He looked down at the dress she was wearing, as if to prove his point. But his eyes lingered too long on her exposed limbs, if he wished to be the arbiter of propriety.

She reached out and slapped his arm to draw his intention back to her face. 'This is a costume. And as for the rest? You seem intent on blowing innocent mistakes into character defects.'

'Innocent mistakes like selling your maidenhead to strangers?'

'Surely that is no worse than buying someone's virtue,' she countered. 'Or running the sort of club where such things go on. You are hardly a shining example of morality if you are here, encouraging others to bad behaviour.'

'And you are too childish to be allowed out of the nursery if you cannot stop obsessing over a ballroom snub,' he countered. 'If it is not just to vex me, then I demand to know what you are doing here, practically naked, and offering your innocence to the highest bidder.'

For a moment, she was lost for an answer. If he was truly so concerned with virtue, he might be the sort of man who would help a lady in distress. Perhaps, if she told him the true reason for coming here, he might be an ally in explaining to her father how desperate she was to avoid this marriage.

Or, since he was here and in charge of the debauchery, he might be no better than Nash.

'Perhaps it is as it appears,' she said, abandoning hope. 'I am here for the excitement, just as the rest of the guests are.'

'Then I am happy to oblige,' he said. 'I will ravish you, right here, if that is what you wish.' He pushed her up against the nearest wall, as if ready to carry out his threat. But the care he took not to touch her bare skin as he did it left her sure that it was nothing more than an attempt to scare her.

'Once you have finished, will you speak to me if we meet on the street?' she asked with a sigh. 'Since you already treat me as if I have done something that renders me beneath contempt, I fail to see what difference it will make.'

He stepped away from her and threw up his hands in frustration. 'That is not the correct response at all. When a man threatens your honour, you are supposed to beg for your freedom.'

She stared up at him. 'If you are truly a threat, I doubt begging will do me any good.'

'If?'

'We have been alone for some minutes,' she said. 'I am as yet untouched.'

'That could change at any moment,' he reminded her.

'Perhaps, if you were anyone else,' she said, rolling her eyes. 'But you are the most puffed-up and proper man in England and not at all the sort of fellow who would deflower a young lady of good birth in a public place.'

'This club is private,' he said.

'But it would not be an easy secret to keep. Touch me and I will tell my father what you have done to me. He would have us up the aisle and married by week's end. If you did not like me at Almack's, think what a trial it would be to have a lifetime of my company.'

'Or I could simply reveal your identity and ruin you before you do so yourself,' he said, answering threat for threat. 'Then your father would pack you off to the country to rusticate and I would not be bothered with you for the rest of the Season.'

It was a perfect solution! She could imagine nothing better than to be sent back to their country home in disgrace and forced to live away from the censuring eyes of the *ton*. If her stepmother stayed in London, there would be no one to scold her for getting mud on her hem, or insist that she conform to rules she'd had no part in making to please men she had no desire to attract.

But such a happy retreat offered no guarantee that Nash would not follow her. More likely, her unwanted suitor would use her total failure in town as an excuse to redouble his efforts to win her. And if she was alone, there would be no one to protect her from his advances. 'I would prefer you didn't,' she said at last.

'If your preferences mattered to me, I would take that under consideration,' he said. 'But it is my job to see that this establishment runs in a well-ordered manner. I cannot simply allow virgins to wander freely about in it, harassing the patrons and risking their reputations on a lark.'

'I was not harassing anyone,' she said. Even if she had been, she would not be returning here to do it. The trick she had just attempted would not work twice. She would have to find another way to rid herself of Sir Nash.

'Then what was your intention?' he repeated, still waiting for an explanation.

'She came to cheat me out of what I deserve.' Sir Nash's voice cut the conversation like a slime-covered knife. As usual, his approach was as silent as his presence was unwelcome. He had removed his mask and was looking at her as if she should be surprised by his appearance, rather than expecting to find him.

'Bowles.' Did Mr Challenger grow larger as he greeted the other man? Or was it simply that he had stepped closer to her in protection? In any case, he looked no happier to see Sir Nash than she did.

'Georgiana thinks that if she barters away her honour, I will take a disgust of her and retract my suit.' The smile he turned on her was as odious as any he had given her in the past. 'You did not suspect that I would be in the very room with you, bidding on that which you choose to squander.'

She opened her mouth to inform him that she had not just suspected, she had been sure of it, and then closed it again. The less he knew about her plan, the better. 'You have no idea what I meant to do,' she said with a contrary toss of her head.

'Perhaps not. But I know what you have accomplished,' he said, grinning in triumph. 'By morning, I shall see that all of London knows what you have done here. And that includes my cousin and your father.'

What all of London thought of her did not matter, nor did she care about her stepmother.

But she could not bear it if her father heard of this incident. It might kill what little feeling he still had for her. 'What would it gain you to do such a terrible thing?'

'I will have no reason to, if you do as your family wishes and accept my offer of marriage. Once the announcement is in *The Times*, we will never speak of this again.'

'That will not be possible.' Mr Challenger had been so quiet during their interchange that his interruption caused them both to jump.

Nash turned to him. 'The matter is between the lady and myself, Challenger. Your opinion is not required.'

'On the contrary.' The other man smiled confidently and placed himself squarely between her and Sir Nash. 'You are operating under several misapprehensions. The first is Miss Knight's reason for attending the club tonight.'

At the dramatic pause that followed this, even Georgiana leaned in, eager to hear what was to come next.

'Enlighten us,' Nash said with a cold glare.

'She was not here to barter her innocence to a stranger. She sold it to me.' Then he turned to her with a smile that would melt the reservations of the most frigid virgin and pulled her into his arms, toying with a lock of her hair. 'I told you it was unwise for us to play such games at Vitium et Virtus. As tantalising as I find this little trick you pulled tonight, it calls too much attention to our relationship.'

'Your relationship.' Sir Nash sounded as if he could not decide whether to be sceptical or annoyed. But George was far too preoccupied with the feeling of being pressed firmly into the body of Frederick Challenger to care what Sir Nash thought about it.

Mr Challenger broke the lustful gaze he had been giving her to frown at Sir Nash. 'Our betrothal is, as yet, a secret from her family. But that makes our bond no less permanent.'

'You?' If Sir Nash's response was incredulous, he was no more surprised than George herself.

'Can you think of a better explanation for Miss Knight's presence here?' Though Mr Challenger delivered the question with a tone of dry sarcasm, it was far more likely that he was thinking the same thing to himself.

'Well...' Nash looked from one to the other of them, obviously not convinced.

'It is not as if she came here to surprise you,'

Challenger said, dismissing her actual plan as impossible. And now that it had gone horribly wrong, it did seem ridiculous. But as long as her mistake did not end up forcing her into the arms of Nash Bowles, it would be an embarrassing success.

She gave not a word to confirm or deny. Instead she sighed and leaned into Mr Challenger's body, nestling there as if it were the most natural thing in the world to be held by a virtual stranger. And it did feel rather nice. His embrace was neither too tight nor too loose and the breath that was ruffling her hair was pleasant.

Perhaps she had needed his protection. At the sight of them together, Sir Nash seemed to swell in his indignation like some disgusting sea creature. 'You are playing a dangerous and foolhardy game, Miss Knight, if you think to partner with this man instead of me. Do you not know the reputation of the Challengers? Surely your father does not wish you to marry into such a rakehell family. And this man is the worst of the lot. Just look at where he is.'

'He is in the same place as you,' Georgiana pointed out quietly. 'I see no difference.'

'There is one and it is significant,' Nash shot

back. 'I am but a patron here, but Frederick Challenger is one of the owners. He is the master of the revels tonight. If you do not wish to give yourself into the hands of a despoiler of innocents, then avoid him at all costs. There can be no greater one than he.'

'Unlike some men, I do not take what is not freely given.' The look he gave Nash told Georgiana quite clearly that, even amongst unrepentant sinners, there were some lines that could not be crossed.

'Georgiana.' Nash turned to her now, holding out a hand as if he could coax her back to his side. But the benign smile that accompanied the gesture was followed by a brief, downward gaze to stare at her body.

It was then that she remembered her state of undress and the fact that the original plan had not included removing her mask. This time, she made no effort to hide her shudder at his gaze.

Without waiting for a request, Mr Challenger stepped away from her and seized a cloth from a nearby table, tossing it about her shoulders, hiding her from view. Then with a manner as dire as death, he pointed a finger at Sir Nash. 'In the future, you will refer to the woman at my side as Miss Knight. At least until such time as she does me the honour of becoming Mrs Challenger. Then, you will not speak to her at all.'

'That day will never come,' Nash said, almost shaking with rage. 'I will talk to my cousin over this. We had an understanding.'

'You do that,' Mr Challenger said. 'But one thing that you will not do is remain in this club a moment more. Collect your hat and be on your way, or I will have Snyder help you to the door.' This was followed with the sort of cold, satisfied smile that assured everyone near that this was less a request than a threat.

'This is not the end, Challenger. This is not the end.' But it looked final enough to Georgiana. Sir Nash was backing towards the door as if afraid to take his eyes from the man next to her. Then, with a swish of the black cape that he wore, he was gone.

And once again, she was alone with Mr Frederick Challenger.

Chapter Three

When he was sure Sir Nash was gone, he released his hold on her and his warm expression returned to disapproval. 'Well?'

'Thank you for making him go away,' she said, her nerve failing her in the face of such a large, angry man.

'Do not thank me. I did not do it for you,' he said. 'I cannot abide that fellow. He cannot seem to manage a visit here without doing something so foul that I have to turn him out. If you had a jot of sense you would not have come here, to risk falling into his clutches.'

In the face of this fresh condemnation, she felt as young and foolish as her stepmother thought her to be. Then, she remembered that Mr Challenger had spent the whole of their limited acquaintance thinking such things about her, with no basis in fact. 'My behaviour was the result of desperation,' she said firmly, looking him in the eye. 'My father and stepmother are all but forcing me to marry Sir Nash and I find him repellent. I thought if there was some way I could prove to them how awful he was…'

'So you came here to find him,' Challenger said. 'And just what did you mean to do once you had?'

She could not reveal the whole of her plan without announcing Ben's part in it. If he lost his position because of her foolishness, how could she forgive herself? 'I thought to scream for help,' she said, wondering if it would have worked. 'When someone came to my rescue, I would demand that he be a witness against Sir Nash to my father.'

'Or you could have drawn a crowd and not a rescuer. You could have been ravished for sport by the very man you thought to entrap, while the worst of the *ton* looked on and laughed.' His voice rose, as if he thought she was some underling who had to stand for his punishment. 'Once he had what he wanted, you'd have had to beg for the honour of the marriage you did not want to keep from being cast into the gutter with the rest of the fallen women.'

'Then what Nash said about you was true,' she responded, raising her volume to match his. 'If you own such a place and would have allowed that to happen, you are as bad, or worse, than any who come here.'

His mouth snapped shut, as though he could not figure out how to respond.

'For your information, he'd have married me no matter what had happened,' she said, crestfallen. 'I think he has debts. My stepmother speaks disapprovingly of his gambling even as she tries to arrange our marriage. He wants my father's money as much as anything else he might get from me.'

'I seriously doubt that.' Mr Challenger gave another sweeping glance up and down her body, as though it was possible to see through the tablecloth that hid it.

After weeks of studiously ignoring her, she was unsure of what to make of his sudden interest. She did her best to disregard it despite the strange tingling she felt at the passage of his eyes. 'Well, your interruption has prevented anything bad from happening tonight. If you will excuse me…' She turned toward the door.

He gave a single, sharp laugh in response.

'And now, you mean to go home as if nothing has changed.'

'What else can I do?' she said, trying to smooth the tablecloth into the semblance of a respectable garment.

'Go on, then.' He smiled, gesturing toward the door. 'If you really think that is a good idea.'

His maddeningly smug tone raised the hairs on the back of her neck. She hated being lectured to like a foolish child. She hated it doubly so when she suspected that she deserved it. 'All right, then. Say what you mean to. You are itching for the chance to scold me and I will not deny it to you. Why can't I just go home? Do you still mean to ravish me?' She had meant it as a joke, but once the words had passed her lips, they seemed to hang in the air between them on a cloud of musk.

'You will go home, untouched,' he said, in a reasonable tone that belied any knowledge of a change in the atmosphere. 'But it will be quite impossible for either of us to pretend that this incident did not happen.'

'Do you mean to tell my father?' she asked in a small voice. The story would sound no better delivered by Mr Challenger than it would from Sir Nash.

'I will not have to. Bowles will be there at first light to do it for me.'

Of course. He would come to press for an immediate approval of his suit. He would portray her as a wayward hoyden and himself as a rescuer from near disaster. 'I have made it worse,' she said, miserably.

'Indeed,' he said, not bothering to spare her feelings. 'And dragged me into it as well. I will have to answer for our secret engagement and our sexual game playing in a club frequented by the more louche half of the *ton*.'

'Oh, dear.' She did not like the man, but she had never intended to include him in her personal problems. Then she remembered the conversation that had just occurred. 'I did not ask you to lie for me.'

'Nor did you denounce me when I did,' he reminded her. 'You were more than willing to hide in my shadow and allow me to take the blame for this debacle. Now you know what you must do to make it right.'

'In truth, I do not.' There was not a way forward that did not lead to disaster.

Mr Challenger dropped to his knee before her. 'Miss Knight, would you do me the honour of accepting my offer of marriage?'

She had heard the phrase, 'without a trace of irony'. This must be the opposite of it. The proposal was delivered without a trace of sincerity. And yet, he did not rise. He stared at her, grim-faced, awaiting an answer.

'But, I do not want to marry you,' she said, staring back at him incredulous.

'Nor do I want to marry you.' If possible, his expression became even more threatening. 'But as you said before, if word of this gets out, I will be called to offer for you. I see no other way to save both of our reputations.'

'Your reputation?' Did men even have them? Of course they did. But she was sure that it did not mean the same thing as it did for girls.

'If you do not marry me, I will be seen as the villain who threatened you, a seducer of innocents. Bowles, on the other hand, will be cast as your rescuer. In either case, your future is set. You will have to marry one of us to avoid ruin.' The statement was followed by the audible grinding of teeth. 'Please, my dear Miss Knight, allow me to be the lesser of two evils.'

The idea was insane. 'But then, we would be married,' she reminded him. 'For ever,' she added, when the first statement seemed to have no impact upon him.

'That is the way it normally works,' he agreed. 'You must have understood the risk when you undertook this desperate mission. As I told you before, if you do not marry me, then you shall wed Bowles.' He looked at her for the length of a breath, then added, 'For ever.'

'For ever,' she repeated. It sounded so final. Eventually, she had known she would have to marry someone. She'd just never imagined it would be to a man who had never been willing to give her the time of day, much less a proposal. But marriage to Nash would be every bit as final and infinitely more horrifying.

Mr Challenger gave an impatient huff, as if it had never occurred to him that the woman he offered for would not accept him without question. 'I do not like the idea any better than you do. But if we are reasonable about the business, we need have very little to do with each other, once we are married.'

'And that is what you consider a proper match,' she said. Even at their worst, her father and Marietta had a better union than that.

He continued, oblivious to her criticism. 'I am a second son. It is not as if I am required to produce an heir. I did not intend to marry. I have no interest in tying myself to a single woman until death. But as long as you do not get in the way of my life, I see no reason why I should not. And it will prevent my sister-in-law from trying to match me up with someone in the future.' Now he was smiling at this small advantage.

'I am glad you are warming to the idea,' she said. He had no right to be happy about a reversal of fortune that would leave her shackled to an annoying stranger.

'We will get a special licence and be married by week's end. After a brief period of celebration, you may retire to my country home, free of the attentions of Bowles.'

And now, he was organising her life. 'I have not said yes,' she reminded him.

'It would be foolish to say no,' he replied.

Perhaps so. But she wanted to say it, all the same.

That was not true. She wanted to shout the word directly into his smug face. She had disliked him from the first moment she'd seen him. Or the second moment, at least. When she had looked across the room at him that first time, she had thought him handsome, heroic, and sophisticated. Then, Marietta had ruined

it and he'd proved he was also arrogant, snob-
bish, and dictatorial.

'If you do refuse me, there is always Nash
Bowles,' he reminded her again in that mock-
ingly reasonable voice she might be hearing
every day for the rest of her life, since she
could think of no other way out of this mess
than the one he had presented to her.

'Nothing would be as bad as marrying Sir
Nash,' she agreed. 'Not even marrying you.'
She could not resist adding the final riposte
and was pleased to see the flash of annoyance
in his eyes.

'You are no gift, either,' he said, not bothering with courtesy. 'But if you will promise to
leave me alone afterward, I am willing to do
the right thing and save you.'

He spoke as if she was a gnat to be waved
away, or an annoying child who needed to be
sent back to the nursery. 'I am willing to accept,' she said, holding her head high and giving him a cold look that would tell him he was
twice as bothersome as she could ever be. 'If
you will swear to leave me alone as well.'

His eyes narrowed. 'Do not worry yourself,
Miss Knight. I have no intention of disturbing
your privacy.' There was a significance in his

tone that she did not fully understand. It was as if her request had actually hurt him in some way that all her other insults had not.

She gave him what she hoped was a worldly smile, that he might think she had intended what had just changed between them. But, in truth, she did not. It probably had something to do with the things he'd threatened her with when he'd rescued her, if one could even call that a rescue.

Did married people ravish each other? That did not sound right. She could not imagine her father and stepmother ever did. And she was quite sure she did not want to ravish Mr Challenger.

There were paintings on the walls of this very room that showed scenes similar to those on Sir Nash's snuffbox. But they had to be exaggerations. There were far too many satyrs involved and she seriously doubted that the men of London were actually hiding cloven hooves inside their boots.

Her future husband had turned his back on her speculating and walked to a corner of the room to pull on a bell rope. He did not turn back to her as they waited for the arrival of the servant he'd summoned, leaving her nothing more than silence and a view of his rigid spine and squared shoulders. If he would only relax, just a little, she'd have admired the masculinity of his frame. But at the moment he looked less like an embodiment of strength and more like a man who had just been caned and was braced to take the next blow without flinching.

By the time a maid appeared, the rigidness he displayed had passed to George like an infection. If they did not find some way to manage with each other, when the time came to marry, they would look more like waxworks than human beings.

Mr Challenger turned and addressed the maid with military stiffness. 'Rose, take Miss Knight to the dressing rooms and find her clothing appropriate for a lady. Then see to it that Snyder gets her out of the club and away before anyone knows of her presence here.'

The girl gave a quick curtsy of assent.

Mr Challenger turned back to her with a smooth half pivot. 'I will call on your father in the morning. Once I have his assent, I will take care of the licence and the matter will be settled in no time.' Even though they were only in the presence of a servant, he offered a deep bow. It had none of the irony that his earlier proposal had held. But there was a mechanical quality to the movement that made her think of the tin man who appeared on the hour out of their mantel clock back home. 'Until I see you again, Miss Knight.'

'Mr Challenger.' She imagined herself as the tin girl that came out of the other side of the clock to meet him, offering the same perfectly controlled curtsy. But as she dipped, she lost her grip on the tablecloth she was still wearing and revealed far too much leg than was proper.

Frederick Challenger's control slipped in response. A quick flick of the eyes downward was followed by a glance heavenward and a tight grimace of disapproval.

Before he could unbend enough to complain aloud, she gathered the cloth close about her again and hurried out of the room after the maid.

Chapter Four

'She is late.' Fred checked his watch for what seemed like the hundredth time and glanced towards the closed front doors of the church and the empty pews that should have contained the bride's family. Only the presence of his two oldest friends prevented him from leaving the chancel and hunting the woman down.

'Only by five minutes,' Oliver Gregory's sympathetic smile flashed in the dimness of the church, seeming even brighter against the darkness of his skin.

The five minutes before a battle felt like a lifetime, as if the mind was trying to savour what might be the last moments of life. Perhaps the same was true today, as he bid farewell to his freedom.

Whether it was five minutes or five years, it did not make Georgiana Knight's behaviour any less annoying. 'She has had nineteen years to prepare for her wedding day. You would think she would be early. Punctuality is vital in any operation.'

'Perhaps in the army,' Jacob Huntington said, as he rubbed the bridge of his nose. The ducal ring of Westmoor, which had recently fallen to him, glinted in the light shining through the stained-glass windows of the chapel. He seemed to feel the weight of it and lowered his hand to twist it on his finger as if it gave him discomfort to wear it. Then he spoke. 'You have sisters, do you not? You must have learned by now that women play hob with timetables.'

'That does not mean I have to like it,' Fred said gruffly. He did not have to like any of this. Not the wedding, nor the bride, nor the sudden upending of his life. Nor did he appreciate being forced to buy breakfast for people he took pains to avoid at any other time. He glanced at his own family, gathered on the other side of the church like storm clouds on the horizon.

It was a tiring proposition at the best of times to see them all together in the same place. The Challenger family motto was *incautus futuri* and they seemed to take pleasure in living up to it. Careless of the future and heedless of consequences, his parents and siblings were prone to excesses, affairs, and embarrassments in public, and arguments and grudges in private. Alone and in pairs, they were bad. *En masse* their bad judgement magnified to astounding proportions.

Perhaps it was good that the Knights had not yet arrived, so he might deal with a few of the problems unwitnessed. His sister-in-law, Caroline, was waving at him, the lace handkerchief in her hand fluttering like the wings of a trapped bird. Without so much as a smile he turned from her, offering the sort of deliberate cut that he had once given to the woman he was about to marry. Perhaps, some day, he could explain to Georgiana the reasons for his behaviour. But it would not be at the front of a church on his wedding day. Fred meant to treat the ceremony with the respect it deserved. If war broke out amongst the Challengers, the first shot would not be fired by the groom.

But it seemed his older brother had no such qualms. Since Fred had refused to come to their pew, Francis had abandoned his wife and was pushing past his friends to speak with him. Fred readied for the handshake he was about to receive and the words of filial advice that were in no way necessary.

Instead, Francis touched his sleeve in an importunate gesture that was all too familiar. 'Will we be starting soon? There is an auction at Tattersall's this afternoon and I do not want to miss it.'

'I cannot marry until the bride arrives,' Fred replied, unsure of who annoyed him most.

'Perhaps she has decided to cry off,' Francis said, ever the optimist. 'I told you to book St. George's for the ceremony. Girls want all of London to know that they are marrying. What is the point of bothering if the ceremony is in some out-of-the-way chapel that attracts no notice?'

If, as Fred suspected, Georgiana Knight was like all the other girls in London, she was in for a lifetime of marital disappointment. He had no intention of catering to her every whim. St. George's was too large, too loud, and too expensive. It was also so popular that even more people would notice the nuptials and remark on the suddenness of them, which was the last thing he wanted.

But according to Francis and his wife, there was no point in doing anything if the world was not gawping in amazement at it. His brother was a true dandy, with a collar so high that he could hardly turn his head and breeches so tight that the world was left wondering how he managed to bend his knees to walk. Caroline dressed in kind. The gown she had chosen today was trimmed in so much lace that it appeared she meant to outshine the bride. When she saw his disapproving glance in her direction, her smile brightened and the waving began again, proving she was as eager for his attention as ever and just as obtuse of his opinion of her.

He made another deliberate turn away and replied to his brother, 'Georgiana's parents were married in this church.' Then he remembered his desire for decorum. Losing his temper with the family only made them worse. He took a breath. 'Georgiana chose the place herself. She has no reason to spite me over it.' It was probably too much to hope that the girl had decided the whole thing was a bad idea and decided against it. But if he meant to carry through with this marriage, he must stop hoping, even in the privacy of his own thoughts, that there was a way out of it.

'She will be here, momentarily,' he said, with as much confidence as he could manage.

'Excellent,' Francis said, finally reaching out to shake his hand. 'And, while I have your attention…'

'How much?' Fred said, before his brother could finish.

'Twenty quid,' Francis replied. 'Just until my luck has turned.'

It was moments like this when Fred was glad he had already received his portion of the estate. The heir to their father's title was likely to run through everything that he had and more. 'Ten,' Fred replied, relieved that the Knights would not see him emptying his purse for a brother who could not manage to stay away from the gaming tables.

As Francis returned to take his seat, Fred glanced past him at the rest of the family. At the moment, his mother was trying to rouse his dozing father by proclaiming with ever-increasing volume her own opinions of the impending marriage. 'The influence of the Bowles family cannot be a good thing on the character of a formative girl. I hope Frederick keeps her well in hand or she will disgrace us all.' The first part of the sentence was quite probably true, but the rest was painting it too brown.

His mother had no right to question the birth and upbringing of others. Francis was a wastrel and at one time Fred had been no better. But he'd eschewed his past wildness to set a good example for their younger siblings. His brother Christian was barely out of university, and dangerously high-spirited.

He had three sisters still in the schoolroom: Mariah, Sarah, and the unfortunately named Josephine. When she'd been born, Mother could not be bothered with the fact that they had been at war. No matter how she fancied the name, his youngest sister reminded everyone of the Empress of France. Of course, neither had she been bothered to find lovers that resembled Father. After his own birth, the family resemblance varied widely from child to child. Though Father had acknowledged them all, when the lot of them were lined up side by side, it was difficult to ignore the truth.

'We have lost him, again.' Jake was waving a hand in front of his face, trying to regain his attention.

'He is distracted by things that concern him more than they do the rest of us,' Oliver said, dismissing his family problems with a shake of his head. 'Do not worry, my friend. We are here to stand by you, just as we always have been.'

'I think, as best men, it is our duty to protect you from the family of the bride, should they ever arrive,' Jake added.

'Or to help you escape them and the bride as well,' Oliver added. 'There is a rumour that she was seen at the club last week.'

Fred could guess where the rumour had started. Now that he had been thwarted, Bowles meant to do what damage he could.

'That is the last place I'd have expected to find a marriageable young lady,' Oliver prodded gently.

'Or a gentleman inclined to marry,' added Jake. 'Especially if that gentleman was you. We did not think, when you chose a bride, that we would read her name in *The Times* along with the rest of London.'

They were right to be hurt that he had not told them before posting the announcement. There had been no secrets between the three of them, since the day they'd met at Eton. But until the girl was properly married and safe from scandal, the truth of their meeting was not his to reveal. Fred did his best to manufacture a happy, bridegroom's smile. 'You have both complained that I lacked spirit for the festivities at the club. Now you know the reason. My heart was engaged.' Though he had not meant to use it on his friends, the lie came surprisingly easy to him. Now that it was started, he could not seem to return to the truth. 'As for her presence there? She meant to surprise me.'

But such behaviour made his intended sound less than virtuous. If he had been marrying in truth, would he have allowed his fiancée to take such a risk? He liked to think he would have resisted temptation until the wedding night. Instead, he was going to resist indefinitely. 'She was a little idiot to be there at all,' he added, not wanting to seem too approving of the visit.

'All the more reason to marry her,' Jake said drily.

'I had to offer for her, after that,' Fred added. But that made him sound desperate. Trapped. And he had just called the supposed light of his life an idiot.

Finally, he gave up and offered something surprisingly close to the truth. 'If I hadn't married her, she'd have ended up marrying Nash Bowles, as her family intended.'

'A fate worse than death,' Oliver agreed with a theatrical shudder.

'Or you,' Jake seconded.

From across the church, his mother's voice echoed yet another unneeded opinion. 'I do not see why he chose to marry this girl. A viscount's daughter is no catch at all when there is a duke's sister waiting single in his immediate set.'

Jake stiffened in shock. Then he relaxed again, choosing to ignore the gossip about his beloved Eleanor. Jake's sister was a dark and quiet beauty, and the mother of a five-year-old girl. The family declared her a widow. But though her surname had changed there had been no mention of a husband by his friend, or even a man that his sister had courted long enough to explain the presence of the child.

Fred shot a quelling glare in his mother's direction which went unheeded, as usual. But the point was moot. Even if he'd wanted to marry Jake's sister, he doubted his friend would have sanctioned the match. They knew far too much about each other to spoil a friendship by becoming family. And he had offered for her, just once, when he'd felt the family was in need of someone to claim the child and hush the rumours. He had been resoundingly refused and they had never spoken of it again.

No matter what the world thought of it, Eleanor gave no indication that she wished to be rescued from any kind of scandal and he had been faintly relieved not to have thrown his lot in with a woman he hardly knew.

Now he had done it anyway. Apparently, he grew no wiser with time. 'Having a wife will not change my life so very much, I am sure,' Fred said, trying to reassure himself. 'Once the honeymoon is over, she will be retiring to my house in Surrey and I will be staying in London.'

His friends were staring at him as though he had gone mad in midsentence. Perhaps too much truth was not a good thing. 'I will visit her on weekends, of course,' he added, not wanting to sound unfeeling.

'So you mean no alteration in lifestyle?' It was hard to tell if Oliver was disappointed by this, or reassured. 'I thought you claimed to have grown tired of the club since returning from Waterloo.'

'Not tired, precisely,' Frederick hedged. 'We have been running the place since uni-

versity. And I thought your responsibilities...'
He glanced to Jake.

His friend, whom he should now be calling
Westmoor, passed a hand over his forehead as
if it were so easy to wipe away the evidence of
the previous night's excess. He had been spending far too much time at Vitium et Virtus with
both the ledger books and the brandy bottle. 'I
will mind my business and you mind yours.'

'Or we shall both meddle in Fred's life,
just as we planned,' Oliver said to distract the
brooding Duke. Then he looked to Fred with
a grin. 'There is a new dancer at the club. She
has ginger hair and a kiss like sweet cinnamon.
If you change your mind, it is not too late for
us to create a diversion...'

Were his true feelings so obvious, or was
this another of Oliver's attempts to cheer him?
If the latter, it was not working. 'You know
damn well that I cannot run at this late stage
without ruining both the girl and myself.'

'Language,' Jake chastised, his smile returning. 'We are in a church, after all. And we
know how you hate scandal.'

'Which is why we should not have brought
you this.' Oliver reached into his pocket for a
flask, passing it forward.

They were right. He loathed scandal. He should not have taken the sip of brandy that they were offering, but he needed a drink. He had not expected to have battlefield nerves over something as unimportant as his own wedding.

'It is perfectly normal to be a bit on edge. We all are,' Jake reminded him. 'After all, you are the first of us to enter that *undiscovered country* from whose bourn no traveller returns.'

Fred looked at him in puzzlement.

'Marriage,' Oliver supplied.

'I believe Hamlet was referring to death,' Fred said, finally able to manage a smile.

'One of us has likely taken that journey already,' Jake said, looking more dour than usual.

'We do not know that,' Oliver said quickly. 'Nicholas is missing. That does not mean he is dead.'

'There was a prodigious amount of blood,' Jake reminded him.

'But if it were a robbery, surely the thief would have taken his ring.' Oliver produced it from his pocket, holding it out. Usually it was kept in a gilded box in the club's private suite and Fred was surprised to see it.

'If Nick meant to leave his old life behind, for whatever reason, it makes perfect sense that he would have abandoned an identifying piece of jewellery.'

Fred stopped himself before snapping that it was in bad taste to bring a *momento mori* to a wedding. But it might be nothing of the kind. As Oliver had said, they could not be sure that their friend was dead.

The alternatives were almost worse. If the blood was not his, whose had it been? Had their friend disappeared to escape a hangman's noose? Fred would have thought that, had it been anything less than murder, Nick would have come to his three best friends for help.

'It is all we have left of him now,' Jake said, staring at the ring. 'We were together at the start. We should be together now, if only in spirit. He would have wanted to be here for you, standing at your side with the rest of us.'

To be honest, some small part of Fred had hoped that, once the announcement appeared in the paper, Nicholas Bartlett might show up in the church, as suddenly and unexpectedly as he had disappeared almost six years ago. Fred had been in Portugal when he'd got the news.

One night, Nick had been at the club, just as always. The next morning, the only evidence of him they'd found was a puddle of blood in the alley behind the club and Nick's signet trampled into the mud.

At the sight of the ring, Fred thought what he'd always thought, when Nick was remembered.

If I had been here, it would not have happened. Whatever it was, I'd have stopped it.

He stared at the ring, which normally resided on the seat of Nick's old chair. 'I suppose, since you have brought this, it is time again?'

'It seemed necessary,' Jake said with difficulty. They were surprising words since, of the three of them, Jacob Huntington was the one of them most resistant to dredging up the past with what he deemed a silly ceremony. But he was probably right. If there was ever a day Fred needed all his friends, in body and spirit, it was this one.

'Shall we begin?' he asked.

The other two nodded, suddenly sombre.

'In Vitium et Virtus,' they said in unison.

Jake raised the flask he was holding. 'To absent friends.' He took a drink and passed it to Oliver.

'Be he in heaven or hell—' Oliver drank and passed the flask to Fred.

'Or somewhere in between—' Fred added, taking a drink.

'Know that we wish you well,' Jake finished, holding the ring out in his closed fist.

The pair of them reached out, covering his hand with their own. They stood for a moment in silence before parting, almost embarrassed by the display of feeling. Oliver cleared his throat and Jake slipped the signet back into his pocket.

'Partaking of spirits in a church?'

Apparently, they had been too preoccupied with the past to notice that the bride and her family had finally arrived. Georgiana's stepmother had caught them drinking and was staring at Fred as if he had just confirmed every horrible story she had heard about his family.

The bride, however, gave a longing look at the flask as it disappeared back into Jake's pocket, as if wishing she could finish what was left.

He hardly blamed her. He had a good mind to request that Jake pass it back so he could share it with her. What were they doing? Even had they felt affection for each other, they had nothing in common. When he looked at her, young, untried, and fresh-faced in a primrose-yellow dress and a coronet of wildflowers, he felt a hundred years old. He was hardly that. He was not yet thirty. But he had seen too much and done too much to have anything at all in common with a green girl.

As she so often was, when he'd seen her in public, Georgiana Knight was pouting, frowning, and snapping at her stepmother, like the child she was. Lady Grinsted was frowning as well as she fluffed the sleeves of the bride's gown and tried to adjust the flowers in her hair. Her father walked two steps behind the pair, purposely oblivious to the drama playing out under his nose.

'Apologise to Major Challenger for our late arrival,' Lady Grinsted said with a brittle smile and a jab of a pin in Georgiana's blonde hair.

'It is Mr Challenger,' Georgiana corrected, staring at the uniform he had chosen for wedding clothes. 'The war has been over for some time.'

'Now is no time to argue semantics,' her stepmother hissed. 'Apologise to him.'

'It is not as if he could start without me,' Georgiana supplied, glaring at him as if daring him to say otherwise. 'And you should be the one to apologise, Marietta. The delay was not my fault. If you would have allowed me to choose my own clothing unchallenged, we would have been here half an hour ago.'

'A day dress that is months old—'

'Barely worn,' the girl interrupted. 'And it favours me.'

'You should have bought a new gown. And woodbine and speedwell for flowers?' Marietta said with a sniff of disgust. 'You look as though you picked them out of the garden.'

'Because I did,' the girl replied.

'There were roses and orchids in the hothouse on the roof.'

'Where they can stay,' Georgiana finished. 'Since you like them, I left them for you to enjoy, now that you are finally to be rid of me.'

Had the delay seriously been about something so trivial as the choice of flowers? She was lovely just as she was, the very picture of the bride he'd have wanted, had he wanted to marry at all. He failed to see what difference it made what she wore. He had promised to marry her and would have done so had she arrived wrapped in a grain sack.

Or in a sheer dress that barely covered her

charms. Why, of all times, was he imagining how she had looked on the night he'd made the offer? The thoughts he'd been having before he'd learned her identity were not appropriate for a church.

Nor were they appropriate if he planned to leave his virgin bride untouched, as she had demanded. It should not matter, for he liked her no better than she did him. But he had never imagined that he would be denied the one clear advantage that one was supposed to gain by marrying. The whole thing was giving him a headache. Or perhaps it was the heavy scent of the Viscountess's perfume, which was redolent of the flowers she had been forcing on her stepdaughter.

He turned to Georgiana, forcing a smile. 'You look perfectly charming.' If everything else was a lie, at least that was true. 'If the guests will take their seats, let us get this over with.'

Chapter Five

As they stood before the altar, Georgiana sneaked a sideward glance at the man next to her, torn between amazement and frustration. It didn't bode well for their future that he could not manage to make it through the ceremony without a drink. Perhaps he was every bit as bad as the rest of his family, who were known far and wide for their excesses in all things.

Nor did it encourage her when he had announced that they needed to 'get it over with' as if he was being forced to take medicine or do something equally unpleasant. He had followed that insult by taking a long look at his watch, to give her one last reminder of their late arrival.

If it had been up to her, they'd have been early and done by now. But, as usual, the preparations had devolved into an argument with Marietta. Perhaps, just once, her step-mother had been right. Standing next to Frederick Challenger, George began to wonder if her choice of gown and flowers had been too plain. While she had chosen muslin and wild flowers, her future husband was resplendent in full military uniform.

She would not let her head be turned. All men looked dashing in a red coat and tasselled Hessians. It was easier to think that than to notice how handsome he was. Though the war had ended some three years ago, the return to civilian life had not made him soft. The body under his uniform seemed to be nothing but muscle and sinew, as ready to vault into the saddle and take up the sword as it had been at Waterloo.

But it had been his face that had drawn her attention when she had first seen him at a ball some weeks before. Even when his brow was furrowed in irritation with her, there was an intelligent light in his dark brown eyes that made her want to know him better. Though his smile today was false, it was still nice to look on. There were no lines about the mouth to indicate habitual frowning. His lips were neither too firm nor too soft. His light brown hair was recently cut and combed smooth. But she could see a faint wave in it, as if it had taken his valet some effort to gain control of the wildness. He was freshly shaved as well, cheeks smooth and clear. As they had moved together to stand before the bishop, she'd got a faint whiff of lime cologne.

He needn't have bothered putting on airs for this sham of a wedding. He had looked just as good at Almack's and even better at the club, where she had seen him without the benefit of coat, cravat, or a razor.

His pleasant appearance did not make up for the fact that he had been annoying in all those places. He had shown nothing but contempt for her since the first time they'd laid eyes on each other. He had laughed at her, mocked her in public, and scolded her when they were alone together at the club. Was it really worth a lifetime's sacrifice to get away from Sir Nash? If not for the threat of him, George would not be marrying a man who disapproved of her every bit as much as Marietta did.

She glanced over her shoulder at her stepmother who was glaring at her from the first pew. No matter what happened from now on, that woman would have no more say in her life or future. She was still furious that George had managed the narrow escape from Sir Nash's impending proposal. The accepted offer from Mr Challenger had resulted in the biggest row of her life. Marietta had alternated between shrieks of rage and fits of tears, demanding that George write a letter of refusal, immediately.

When that had failed, she had begun on Father, hanging on his arm and proclaiming that her cousin's heart would be broken by the jilting of the faithless Georgiana. He must contact Mr Challenger immediately with the news that she was otherwise engaged.

Father had looked from one to the other of them and sighed. Then announced that George was marrying and leaving the house, just as Marietta had wanted. Since it appeared that she had finally found a man she was willing to accept, he had no intention of reopening the matter. Then he had locked himself in the study to avoid further discussion.

As for her own opinions on the marriage? After the initial offer, even Mr Challenger had not enquired on those. The morning after the embarrassing interlude at Vitium et Virtus, he had come to the house and spoken to Father, just as he'd promised.

When he had done with that, he'd stopped to speak to her, where she had been loitering in the corridor outside the study. He had promised to arrange for the licence and announcement and put an allowance at her disposal should she need it for wedding preparations. Then he had given her his direction so she might contact him once the rest of the plans had been finalised.

And that had been that. It had all been arranged through a series of notes passed between the two households. Beyond the stack of curt but polite replies written in a bold, masculine hand, she had not seen him in the flesh, in public or private, since that morning.

He had been conspicuously absent from the routs and dinners she had attended, denying her even the usual aggravation of his censure. She had been left alone to weather the flurry of congratulations for her impending marriage along with the curious questions that often accompanied them. When had they met? When had he offered? How had they managed to carry on a flirtation under the very noses of the Almack's patronesses without anyone in London guessing the truth?

She had smiled brilliantly and lied through her teeth. It would serve Mr Challenger right if word got back to him of their romantic meetings in Vauxhall and unchaperoned moonlight rides. If he had wanted another version of their courtship, he should have been there to help her invent it.

She felt a sudden, sharp elbow in her side. Her soon-to-be husband had caught her woolgathering at the altar. She turned back to the ceremony and saw the expectant look on the face of the bishop. She had missed something, she was sure. 'Could you repeat the question?' she asked, as sweetly as possible.

'Will you, Georgiana Hortensia Knight, take this man…?'

Blast.

Of all the time to let her mind wander, it had to be during the vows.

'I will,' she said, relieved that this bit was over at least.

And now, it was Mr Challenger's turn to answer. He stood beside her, back straight, shoulders squared as if Wellington himself would be delivering the sermon.

Suddenly, there was a snore from the Challenger family pew.

The bishop froze, mid-word, glancing past them at the Earl.

There came another, prolonged snort that ended in a muffled curse.

'Dear Lord, Weston. Of all times.' Perhaps the Countess had intended her remonstrance to be a whisper, but in the cavernous interior of the church it carried like a shout.

'It is damned early to be up and about,' the Earl said in his defence. 'Since he wasted the money on a special licence, we could have done this in the afternoon, when we were all awake.'

'If you had not got so drunk last night, a morning wedding would be no problem.'

Beside them, the Earl's heir tapped once on the floor with his gold-handled walking stick as if the sound of ebony striking the marble floor was in any way a discreet warning. In trying to silence him, his wife let out a hissing noise that rebounded off the vaulted ceiling.

From the next pew, Mr Challenger's younger brother let out an embarrassed sigh and the younger sisters began to giggle, unable to help themselves.

The man beside her took a deep breath, swelling to become even more fearsome and impressive than she'd first imagined. Then he turned with military precision to glare at his family. 'Silence!' He delivered the command in his best battlefield roar.

It was as if the entire congregation had turned to stone. His friends were gaping, open-mouthed. When the effects of the shout wore off, the Earl winced at the pain in his brandy-soaked skull. The Countess looked as if she had just bitten down on a lemon. The rest of the family had fallen into white-faced, wide-eyed, terrified silence.

From beside Mr Challenger, his dark-skinned friend Mr Gregory let out a low chuckle. It was cut short by a sudden elbow to the ribs from the Duke of Westmoor.

Mr Challenger gave them one last glare foul enough to make sure they all remained still. Then he turned back to the bishop and said, in what he probably thought was a calming tone, 'Please proceed.'

The bishop hesitated for a moment more, as if he were standing out in a storm, waiting to see if lightning would strike again. Then the ceremony continued. He was prattling on about love and obedience and several other virtues that George was sure did not pertain to the arrangement that she had negotiated with Mr Challenger.

But for today, she would smile and nod along. She would agree to each question put to her and focus on the only vows that truly mattered. Once they were married, they would leave each other alone.

The plan was simplicity itself and infinitely preferable to being trapped cheek by jowl with a man she did not like. Why, then, did it make her feel so empty to contemplate it? Before she had come to the church, she'd calmed her nerves by remembering that she had no real expectations of what marriage was supposed to be like.

Her parents had been happy, of course. Then, Mother had died. Her father and Marietta were happy, at first. And then, they were not. It was quite possible that true happiness was a fragile thing, not meant to last the lifetime of the union.

But to begin and end a marriage in antipathy seemed so wrong. Perhaps it would be possible for some little bit of affection to grow between them. If she made an effort not to annoy him and he did not speak too often, or cause aggravation to her, they might learn to be comfortable in each other's presence. It would be nice if he accompanied her when she received an invitation to a ball. Even better if he was willing to partner with her in a dance or two. If she tried it, she might like walking at his side as well as she had several other less handsome but more personable men she'd met this Season.

But there would be no children.

The realisation brought with it a strange emptiness. She had always assumed that, some day, she would have them. What better way was there to know that one was truly grown up? When she became a mother, people would stop treating her as a child. But Mr Challenger had stressed that he did not need an heir. That meant that they would not be performing whatever mysterious acts resulted in children. And he would never think of her as anything more than a useless child.

'You may kiss the bride.'

Her cogitation came to an abrupt halt. The ceremony was over. At the encouraging of the bishop, he was about to do something that she had not allowed any man to do in her life. He had touched her shoulder and was turning her to him. Now he touched her chin so she had no choice but to look up at his face.

His eyes truly were amazing, so dark and

deep that she could stare into them for ever and never grow tired of the view. And for a moment, she was sure that her fears were baseless. Everything would work out between them. At least for a single moment, she would hold the full, romantic attention of a gallant soldier, a worldly and not too gentlemanly gentleman, a near perfect specimen of masculinity.

She closed her eyes and waited for something that was guaranteed to be a primer-perfect first kiss.

Then, as usual, Frederick Challenger ruined everything.

It was the sort of kiss one gave one's worst aunt when forced to make nice. Or perhaps a sister, when one was still in the schoolroom and hated all females, especially ones in the family. He kissed her as if he had wanted to be anywhere but at the altar with her. He all but proclaimed his unhappiness with the union in front of both his family and hers.

She was sure her cheeks were burning red with embarrassment and not the just-kissed flush she'd been hoping for. Now she had to walk down the aisle with him and pretend that everything was fine. She would have to sit beside him at breakfast, eat cake, and drink champagne, and act as though she had not just made the worst mistake in her life by marrying him.

She should have thrown this first precious kiss away on a flirtation, months ago, instead of saving it for a husband who would never feel anything for her but contempt. At least, then she'd have had a pleasant memory to sustain her through a lifetime of misery.

She must not let this moment become even worse than it already was. She would not let Frederick Challenger or anyone else see how much he had hurt her. As they walked to the registry to sign their names in the book, she raised her chin and willed the burning shame into cold, hard anger. Today, she would accept the felicitations on her marriage with a smile. She would eat her wedding breakfast with relish, even if it choked her.

But when they got home, wherever that place turned out to be, she would make it clear that, no matter what she had said at the altar, hell would freeze before she offered the odious man at her side love, honour, or obedience.

Chapter Six

George toyed with the wilting bouquet in her hands, watching the cascade of flower petals falling on a low table in Mr Challenger's town house. It would be sensible to begin thinking of this as her home as well. After all, her clothing and material possessions were currently being unpacked by servants in the rooms around her. But such an easy adjustment was probably impossible. After less than a day as a wife, she'd had enough of marriage to last her a lifetime.

The wedding breakfast had been as awful as she'd expected it would be. Mr Challenger had been polite enough to the servants at the hotel where the meal was held. But he had not said two words together to his parents or older brother and offered nothing but sharp admonitions to his younger siblings that they mind their manners and not annoy the other guests. And though she had come to them offering warm smiles and congratulations, he had stared through his sister-in-law as if she was not even there.

George had almost come to miss the old, obnoxious Frederick Challenger who would have cut her dead as well. The new one spoke to her with distant courtesy, but refused to look her in the eye as he did so. He made sure that her glass was full and that her plate held the choicest dainties on the table. Then he ate, head down, knife and fork clicking against china as rhythmically as a machine, until the meal was over.

He made the effort to hand her up into the carriage and make sure of her comfort. But he returned to silence on the ride to his home, staring out the carriage window at the passing scenery. If he expected her to be the one to carry the conversation for the rest of their lives, he was sorely mistaken. For all she cared, they would go to their graves without exchanging another word.

His town house in St James's Square was fashionable enough, in a sterile sort of way. Though she'd thought her father's servants to be exemplary, they did not hold a patch to the Challenger household staff. When given a tour by the housekeeper, she found not a speck of dust anywhere in the house and not a single fringe on the rug out of line. When she returned to the sitting room, the tray of cold meats laid out for tea had been cut wafer-thin and rolled into a display of rosettes and leaves that was almost too pretty to eat.

She stole a slice of ham from an edge, chewing. It was a shame she would not be here for long. If the house had belonged to any other man, she might have enjoyed being mistress of it.

Her moment of peace was destroyed by the appearance of her new husband, entering the room at his usual brisk, military pace. She sighed and made a show of dropping her bouquet on the table as she helped herself to another slice of meat. 'Hello, Mr Challenger.'

'Madam,' he said with a sober nod, but added nothing more to hint at his plans for the future.

She abandoned her earlier plan to punish him with silence. There were things that needed to be settled. If he did not broach them, she must. 'We are married now.'

He nodded.

'And I thank you, very much, for freeing me from the risk of marriage to Sir Nash.'

'You're welcome,' he said, walking to a sideboard to pour himself a glass of brandy.

'But I think it is time to discuss my future.' Apparently, she must remind him, for he seemed to be offering no information on his own.

'Your future,' he said, as if surprised that she would be interested in it.

'What happens next?' She'd have wondered the same thing if their marriage had been a normal one. But she doubted that she'd have had to ask it of him. He would simply have smiled and shown her everything she'd wanted to know.

But remembering the kiss in the church, perhaps he did not know either.

He gave her another deep look. Then he drained the glass, set it aside and stared down at the floor, clasping his hands behind his back, turned on his heel and began a slow circumnavigation of the room.

'Will you be finding me rooms?' she prompted. 'Or will the choice be left to me?' Or could she just go back to her father's house in the country as she wished to and pretend that the Season had never happened?

The pacing stopped. 'Rooms?' He looked up and frowned. 'Why the devil would I be doing that?'

'The agreement was that we would live separately,' she reminded him.

'Metaphorically, we will,' he agreed.

'You mean to live separately under the same roof,' she said, shaking her head in disbelief.

'Of course.' He looked back at her with the same incredulous expression she was giving him. 'We agreed that we would not bother each other.'

'You are bothering me right now,' she said, gritting her teeth. 'The only way to prevent annoyance is by living in separate residences.'

'If you think that you can set up housekeeping for yourself less than a day after your wedding, you are even more feather-brained than I thought.'

'It speaks,' she said, clasping her hands together in feigned enthusiasm.

'You know damn well I do,' he growled.

'I was beginning to doubt it,' she said. 'There were more words in that sentence than you have said in hours.'

'Since you have decided to pay better attention than you did during the wedding ceremony, I will continue.'

She sat on the edge of her chair, folding her hands in her lap, like the good little schoolgirl he wanted, and gave him an artificial smile.

'The object of this whole endeavour was to avoid scandal,' he said in the patient tone one would use on an idiot. 'You cannot simply marry me and disappear. We will continue to share a residence for as long as is necessary for the town to lose interest in us.'

'Really,' she said.

He ignored her mocking tone and continued. 'As you may have noticed, I prefer to live my life and run my household by a few simple rules. My wife will be bound by these rules as well.'

'Will I?' she said and rose from her chair to stand before him like a private at attention.

'When we are in public, I expect a certain level of decorum. While the rest of my family is known for its laxity, I am not.'

'Laxity,' she said, rolling her eyes. It was the politest possible way to describe the fact that his mother had been flirting with the footman at their wedding breakfast and his father had been too drunk to notice. 'Do not worry, Major Challenger. I am sure you are the very opposite of lax.' The word 'rigid' came to mind.

He did not even blink at her use of his rank, as though he had always assumed that his wife would recognise he was her commanding officer. 'Now that we are married, I expect you to adhere to the same rules and principals that I do.'

'And what might those be?'

'You will take no excess of alcohol in public or private.'

She reached back to the table at her side, lifted her wine glass, and toasted him before draining it. 'Of course not, Major Challenger.'

'An extra glass will do no harm, on special occasions,' he allowed.

'Thank heavens,' she said and poured more wine, sipping as she spoke. 'Pray continue, Major Challenger.'

'I am more concerned with public indiscretions that might result from drunkenness. I do not like wastefulness or foolishness.'

'Foolishness,' she said, remembering the looks he had given her each time they'd met.

'You must avoid the sort of behaviour that draws all eyes to you in a public place and leads to disapprobation,' he said, dismissing every social faux pas she had ever made as if they were both deliberate and easy to avoid. 'I do not want to see my wife mentioned in the tattle sheets, or to have her become a laughing stock amongst my friends.'

'I will take it under advisement,' she said, finishing her wine in one gulp and setting the glass aside.

'Likewise, you will not squander your allowance on gambling, or flaunt your indiscretions in my face.'

'You must never see me being indiscreet,' she said, sure that it was not what he had meant at all. But since she was not totally sure what he meant by indiscretions, she was not yet sure how to flaunt them.

'Most importantly, you will refrain from going to Vitium et Virtus.'

'That is all?' she said, waiting to see what other stupidity he might spout.

He gave her the same grave nod he had done before.

'Then let me tell you my opinion of your requirements,' she said, her voice rising to a volume that he probably found indiscreet. 'I am not prone to excesses, so I will continue to drink what I like, when I wish to. I have no intention of watering my wine in public just to soothe your groundless fears.'

He was staring at her as if he had never expected her to speak, other than to agree with his nonsense.

'Secondly, you will not be troubled with witnessing my indiscretions. As I reminded you just now, we agreed before this marriage that we would live apart. You will not see me being indiscreet. After today, I hope you will not be seeing me at all.'

'That was not what I meant...' he began.

'Because, despite what you seem to think, the purpose of this marriage was not to avoid embarrassment, it was to avoid Nash Bowles. I do not care what society says about me as long as they do not call me Lady Bowles when they do it.'

'I, however...' He held a finger in the air, ready to lecture.

She gave him no chance. 'Lastly, if I choose to go to Vitium et Virtus again, I see no reason why I cannot. I am a married woman, after all, and not some innocent who needs to watch her reputation at all times.'

'Well, actually...' he began.

'I should be perfectly safe, since my husband is one of the owners. You have spent much time there, yet you are still so full of propriety that I can hardly stand to be in the same room with you.'

'You cannot simultaneously shun my company and go to the place where I spend my evenings,' he reminded her, more incredulous than bemused. 'And you might be married, but believe me, my dear, you are still innocent.'

He was twitting her about the thing she did not know again. But if learning about it meant she had to spend any more time with Frederick Challenger, she would rather die in ignorance. 'I am not so innocent that I do not know what a kiss should feel like.'

She could see by his sudden flush that he was as mortified by their wedding kiss as she had been. Good. He should suffer for it. 'It amazes me that a man who has spent as much time as you have steeping in vice at a place full of nude women and lechers has gained nothing from the experience.'

He was already red with anger, but now he reminded her of a pot ready to boil over.

Then let him do so. It was time that he learned what it was like to be the butt of continual criticism instead of the source of it. 'Perhaps there is someone at your precious club who can explain to you the correct way to kiss a woman. Maybe they have a library with books on the subject. At the very least, you might examine some of the appalling pictures hanging on the walls.'

'Or perhaps I will simply visit with any woman there. There is not a one of them that would deny me erotic companionship, should I ask for it,' he retorted, unable to remain silent.

'Courtesans,' she said, trying to sound knowing rather than hurt by his inevitable infidelity. 'That is an excellent idea. If you pay a woman to be affectionate, she will not dare to tell you that you kiss like a dead fish.'

By the dangerous silence that followed her insult, she knew she had pushed him too far. After what seemed like ages, he spoke. 'I am glad to have your opinion, based on your vast previous experience.' The comment was delivered in an uninterested tone, as if she had expressed a preference for chicken over fish. Why did it raise gooseflesh on her skin?

He took a step closer to her and she had to fight the urge to run. 'So you do not like the way I kiss.'

She did not. But by the look in his eyes now, it would be the height of folly to goad him further than she already had.

'Let me assure you, Georgiana, if and when I want a woman, I do not need to pay for her time. She gives. And I make sure that she is happy to have done so.'

If he looked at them as he was looking at her now, she could imagine any number of women succumbing to whatever he demanded. Why, then, did he not work this magic on her? 'Prove it,' she said.

Before she could regret her dare, he closed the distance between them, took her in his arms, and kissed her.

This.

What he was doing to her was not exactly what she had been hoping for in the church. She had expected that the ceremony would end with a gentle seal of his lips on hers to mark the covenant. It would leave her with the same sort of warm glow that one got standing next to a fire on a cool day.

What was happening now was like dancing around a bonfire, while fireworks burst in the night sky above her head. But she must be dancing naked for she could feel the heat of the flames on every inch of her skin. She wanted to touch herself all over, to see if the heat was real, or imagined. Better yet, she wanted to be touched.

His kiss was not a brief brush of lips, but an open-mouthed frenzy. His tongue was in her mouth and hers in his. It should have been horrifyingly invasive. Instead, she opened her mouth wider to receive more of him, as if searching for a way to take his soul into her own body.

While a part of her felt like dancing, another part of her wanted to relax like a cat in a patch of sunshine. Though their mouths were lost in a tumultuous joining, her body was weightless, boneless, and his to mould like clay. She wanted to be what he wanted, to be made over by him into a new person.

His hands released the grip on her arms and moved up, over her shoulders and down her back. By the time they'd reached her hips, she knew every inch of him, as he did her. And yet, by the burning inside her, she was sure there was more to learn.

Despite the forcefulness of his embrace, she felt safe in his arms. Perhaps, in a moment, he would sweep her up in them and carry her up the stairs and into the bedroom. She was still not quite sure what would happen next. But with each passing moment, she was growing more eager to find out.

Then, just as suddenly, he released her. He was panting for breath and his arms were rigid at his sides as though he could not decide whether to reach for her again or push her away. He looked as angry as ever, but confused as well.

Her breathing was as ragged as his and all her glib words had fled. She couldn't seem to manage more than to blink at him as she waited for his next words.

'I trust I have established that I am experienced enough to be a satisfactory husband. It is a shame that you do not know enough to be a proper wife.'

Had she done something wrong just now that had proved she was not just inexperienced but unteachable? Or did he truly dislike her so much that he would offer such a kiss just to deny her more as a punishment? If that was the truth, she felt even worse now than she had before.

But to show her feelings would give him more ammunition to hurt her with. 'Are you a satisfactory husband?' She affected an annoyed shrug. 'If I follow the guidelines you have set for me, I have had far too much wine to trust my own judgement on the matter. And if you expect me to follow the rest of your silly rules before you declare me proper enough to get another kiss, then I guess we will never know.'

There was another deadly pause. Then he gave a growl of uncontrollable frustration and reached for her again, as if he thought it might be possible to kiss her into agreeability.

Remembering how she'd felt just now, he was probably right. But she had no intention of allowing herself to be so manipulated by a man who only wanted to control her. She darted clear of his grasp, turned to the table, and grabbed the first thing that came to hand: the sad bouquet she had carried to her equally sad wedding. Then she swung it with all of her might at the side of his head.

'Don't you dare touch me, ever again!' The flowers exploded in a cascade of petals and she ran out the door and up the stairs, to lock herself in a bedroom that she had never wanted in the first place.

Chapter Seven

Diplomacy was not Fred's strong suit. It was why the army had suited him so well. By the time a battle arrived, there was no need for discussion. If his superiors had doubts, they kept them to themselves. And they never had to contend with the damaged sensibilities of their men on the morning after.

That might explain the absence of women in the military. But it was not just women that were Fred's problem. He had never been any good at dealing with the excesses of his father and brother, either. While Pater deserved respect for age and rank alone, there was no way he could cede it easily to his idiot brother Francis because of one year's superiority and a direct line to an earldom.

Fred had chafed, argued, and evaded when dealing with people he did not like, even when his friends had hinted that subtlety might rule the day. And though he'd bought his commission to run away from his problems, in Portugal he'd had no choice but to meet challenges head-on and conquer them.

But nothing had prepared him for Georgiana Knight. He had sown the wind with an impromptu marriage. He should not be surprised that the proverbial whirlwind had arrived on the wedding night. After she had crowned him with her bouquet, she had run upstairs and disappeared into her room with a slam of the door that must have been heard all the way to the basement. He had been left alone, picking flower petals out of his hair, sure in the knowledge that the household staff knew their master had been banned from the marital bed.

Not that he'd actually planned to bed her. Not immediately, at least. He had promised her that he would not impose himself upon her. But some part of him had assumed that the situation would change with time. When two people were alone in the same house, things sometimes happened. Why should they not? Congress between a man and a woman was an enjoyable activity. In their case, it was even sanctioned by the church. When the opportunity presented itself, desire would not be a problem. She was not unattractive.

If he was honest, she was more than that. She was really quite lovely. When he had rejected her on their first meeting, he had done so with regret. His taste already ran to tall blondes and only a fool did not like big, blue eyes and full, pink lips.

But it had not been her face he'd remembered, as they stood together at the altar. A stray beam of light had shone through the muslin of her gown and the briefest outline of her shoulder had sent him down a moonlit path of fantasy, remembering how she had looked when he'd rescued her at Vitium et Virtus and what might have happened between them.

Breasts. Not too large, not too small. Firm handfuls of flesh cresting over a skimpy bodice. Pert nipples outlined under gauze that clung so tight to her flat belly her navel made a dark hollow in the fabric.

Legs. Not just a titillating glimpse of ankle. He had seen shapely calves, round hips and thighs that begged to be parted. When her skirt had shifted, he'd had a brief view of the sweet place where they met. Damn Jake and his talk of undiscovered countries. What man would not want to experience *la petite mort* after that particular journey?

He'd felt the same warning stirring in church that was taking him now. The male body's primordial rebellion against common sense at inappropriate times was understandable, if one was a schoolboy. But for a grown man who prided himself on iron control, it was worse than embarrassing. It bordered on the ridiculous.

So he had focused his mind on anything but the woman at his side. He had brooded on his family's behaviour. He'd enumerated the bride's faults. For the first time in his life, he had listened intently to a sermon. By the time the bishop had made the final pronouncement that would bind him to Georgiana Knight for ever, Fred's blood was as cold as the champagne waiting at the breakfast.

Then, he had turned to kiss her.

His calm shattered. She had looked up into his eyes with an expression of such naked longing that his mouth had gone bone dry. He wanted her every bit as much as he had the night at the club. He wanted to seize her and kiss her as he should have then, to explain in a single action the advantages of a physical union between them.

But one did not do such things in public, much less in church. Even in private, he must remember that the girl was a virgin and deserved patience and understanding before intimacy. Most important, she had made it quite clear that she did not want him, no matter what her feelings were at the moment. He would kiss her, of course. He had to. But it must be a proper kiss. A kiss as innocent as she was. And that kiss must make it seem that he did not care as much as he did.

He kissed her. And it was awful. No. He was awful. It had been as if, as soon as the knot was tied, he had forgotten everything he'd ever learned about taking and giving pleasure. He had given her a virgin's first kiss, in fact. A male virgin. A thin-lipped, bone-dry peck that had landed half on her lips and half off, as if he had been afraid to make full contact lest she laugh in his face.

It did not take an experienced woman to recognise such blatant romantic failure. Georgiana had pulled away from him after, red with fury. Even his friends had smiled and shaken their heads in pity, then muttered about wedding-night nerves.

He owed her an apology. He'd even intended

to make one. Then he'd planned to explain the need to share a bedroom in the most innocent possible way to prevent household gossip. He would sleep on the floor while she took the bed. A quick rumpling of the sheets in the morning, and perhaps a spot of blood to reinforce the maid's assumptions about what had happened. In a day or two, he would return to his own room. No one would dare question his comings and goings after.

He had reconciled himself to the fact that the marriage need never be consummated. While it would be embarrassing to admit that he had never bedded his own wife, he was not required to tell anyone the fact. Nor was he so enraptured with tradition that he felt the need to mark her as a possession if they felt no attraction to each other.

But before he could get a word in she had asked about separate living arrangements and he had taken to hectoring her and trying to regain control. In response, she'd continued to goad him until he had lost his temper and his mind.

At least, when he had stopped thinking, the kissing had improved. Their mouths had fit together perfectly, as had their clothed bodies. His manhood had immediately wondered how well they might fit when naked. Virginity was nothing more than a uniquely female sort of ignorance. It was easily solved. And by the sway of her body against his, the slight sighs at the friction of clothing against her body, she seemed like an apt pupil ready for vigorous education.

Then she had hit him with her flowers and locked him out of her bedroom. Who would have thought such a small creature could have so much anger in her? In certain circumstances, it might have been admirable. Women who were passionate in public often carried such emotion to the bedroom with them. He'd been with women who had started arguments just for the opportunity to make up afterwards. Perhaps Georgiana would be the same.

He blinked in surprise. The woman was his wife. The last thing he needed to be speculating about was the nature of her passions. While some might think that such things were exactly the purview of a spouse, one had only to look at his brother to see what happened when men followed their hearts, or, worse yet, their loins, into a lifelong union. The fire Francis had felt for his wife had cooled in less than a year, but the scorn they felt for each other would linger for a lifetime.

He would not make the same mistake in his marriage. Georgiana Knight had been a virtual stranger to him when he'd wed her and so she would remain. Of course, she'd also been a stranger who made no bones about her loathing for him. Unless he wanted the *ton* to find a fresh embarrassment to add to the family scandal sheet, he needed to convince her to pretend affection towards him.

And here was the woman now, entering the breakfast room with the hesitance of one still so unfamiliar with her surroundings that she was unsure what awaited her on the opposite side of each closed door. He felt another pang of embarrassment. Or was it shame? It did not matter how she felt about him or how he felt about her. He would not have treated any other visitor to his home so shabbily that they woke unable to find their breakfast.

He let proper manners take hold of him, rising and turning to greet her. Even if he could not manage to smile, he owed her the same courtesy and civility he'd have given any other lady. 'Georgiana.' He bowed.

'Mr Challenger,' she responded with a cautious inclination of her head.

'Please, come in, sit down.' He pulled out her chair for her, saw her properly seated, and arranged the chocolate pot and toast rack at a convenient distance from her plate before returning to his seat at the head of the table. 'I trust you slept well?'

The silent look she gave him in return spoke volumes. Since she had gone to her room in a rage and quite possibly hungry, he had no reason to make optimistic assumptions about the quality of her rest.

'Was the bed to your liking?' he asked. A brief image of a sleep-tousled Georgiana rising naked from white sheets flashed through his mind and he kicked himself for mentioning bed at all.

'The mattress was satisfactory,' she said, her voice brittle.

'And the room? You may decorate it to your preferences, of course. But is the size and arrangement of it sufficient for your needs?' And what were her needs, or those of any other woman, for that matter? He had no idea.

Her frown deepened to remind him that the bed would be better if it were miles away from whereever he resided. 'It is more space than I require.'

He nodded. This was as good an introduction as any to yesterday's argument. 'Because you have no desire to remain here for long. You wish your own rooms. Or a house, perhaps.'

'But not a large one,' she replied. 'The settlement from my father is generous, but I do not intend to squander it.'

'Of course not,' he said, somewhat mollified. Her frugality might be common ground between them. 'Despite my behaviour yesterday, I have no desire to see you unhappy.' Now he should apologise, but the words stuck in his throat. Since the argument had been from her unwillingness to cede control of the marriage, she should be the sorry one. It was the natural order of things that she follow his lead.

But he had known that she was an unnatural creature from the first. Proper women did not turn up half-naked in sporting clubs. Nor did they trick unsuspecting men into marrying them. Could he really fault her for being consistently inconsistent? 'I am sorry that we argued,' he said at last. That truth did not require him to give any ground.

'And I am sorry if you find me difficult,'

she said, giving him an equally weak contrition.

It would do. He let out a small sigh of relief. 'Then we agree that we wish to make our way through this awkward situation as pleasantly as possible.'

'You speak of our marriage as if it is a bog,' she said, focusing her full attention on the toast in front of her, slathering it with marmalade to the very edges and licking a drip from her finger with the tip of her tongue.

He stared at it and felt his own mouth water. He was giving her table manners far too much attention. Probably because he was not used to being distracted by an attractive female at breakfast. Perhaps tomorrow, he could eat alone, in silence, reading his mail, just as he always did. But today, he needed to speak to her, if he could manage to remember what it was that he'd meant to say.

She was cleaning her other fingers now, with catlike dabs of her tongue. They were almost like small, wet kisses. They would be sweet kisses, because of the jam...

She looked up at him, returning his stare.

He looked quickly back to his own plate which was already empty. He put another kipper on it, not because he was hungry, but because it seemed foolish to be lingering at table with her when he was so obviously finished with his meal.

'Do you view our union as an obstacle?' she said, reminding him of the discussion in progress.

'I view our marriage as a challenge,' he said. There was no point in avoiding the truth. 'But not an insurmountable one. If we work together, we can solve it,' he added.

'What sort of challenge? And why must we do anything together? You made it quite plain that you wanted nothing to do with me.' Did she sound hurt? 'And I want nothing to do with you, either.' She'd added that so quickly he wondered if it was meant to disguise a tender heart.

'Living separate lives is not quite the same thing as having nothing to do with each other,' he said, patiently. 'There will be questions enough about our marriage without making the world think we are enemies.'

'But why should it matter what the world thinks?' she said, her annoyance returning.

He and his friends had said something similar when they'd started the club. But Fred had come to realise that, no matter what he said, he'd felt something quite different when he had watched his family's behaviour. 'It matters to me what the world thinks of us. Since I am your husband, it should matter to you as well.'

It was a simple enough explanation for even a child to understand. He knew what was best and she should abide by his rules. Instead, she looked at him not just with doubt, but with rebellion. 'You think because we have been forced into a union, that your opinion, which did not matter at all to me a week ago, should be the mark upon which I measure all future behaviour.'

'I do.' But why did she make unquestioning obedience sound so unreasonable? 'Since I am not asking for anything more outlandish than a truce between us, perhaps you can enumerate the problems you see with agreeing.'

Perhaps he was learning to be subtle. By the puzzled look on her face, it was clear that she had no good response. Then she said, carefully, 'Just what might such a truce entail?'

'Nothing too terribly onerous,' he assured her. 'We both want to live separately. But I would like to do so without adding to the gossip that is already swirling about our sudden wedding. Interest in us will wane if we attempt to seem like a happy couple, at least long enough for a honeymoon.'

'A month,' she said, taking said moon as a literal measure of time.

He nodded. 'We should be seen in public together over the next few weeks. The Season is almost over. By the end of June, most of the gossips will have gone to Bath or Brighton. At such time, we can adjourn to the country...'

'Or to separate homes,' she finished.

'By next Season, our marriage will be old news. If we maintain multiple dwellings and do not spend all our evenings in each other's pocket, we will be no different from most other couples in London.'

She stared at him for a moment as though weighing advantages and disadvantages before answering, 'Very well. How do you suggest we begin?

'A ride this afternoon, I think. Everyone who is anyone will be in Hyde Park. I suggest we join them.'

Chapter Eight

George's problems with Mr Challenger's truce began almost immediately.

Or was she to think of him as Frederick now that they were pretending to be happy? Somehow it did not seem natural. Perhaps not. It was rare to hear a wife be so informal as to use her husband's given name, though her parents had never spoken with formality at home. The Christian names they'd exchanged were always passed with smiles of such warmth that she'd had no doubt of their love for her and each other.

But now, as she looked at the man next to her, she could not imagine ever calling him anything but Mr Challenger. Or perhaps Major Challenger, since he seemed intent on ordering her about.

His brief bout of reasonableness had hardly

lasted until they'd left the breakfast room. She had responded eagerly to his suggestion of a ride. It was always a relief to throw off some of the strictures put upon her and have a good gallop. But she should have known that his idea of a ride would be nowhere near as exciting as that.

Now, as she stood in the mews at the back of the house, she stared at the horse he had chosen for her with disdain. 'And what is the meaning of this?'

He had already taken to the saddle of a fine Arabian stallion, tugging at his riding gloves to be sure that they offered him a good feel for the reins. 'It is the most appropriate beast that could be hired on short notice. There are few grown women in my family. I do not keep an appropriate mount for a lady.'

She compared the fine blood he was riding to the sad mare that had been chosen for her. 'Are you sure she is strong enough for this? Perhaps I should be the one to carry her.'

'I am sure she is quite up to the task of a ride around the park,' he said, ignoring her sarcasm.

She looked enviously at his horse again, remembering all the times she had been allowed to take her father's Turk out for exercise. 'At least allow me to dispense with the side saddle. Perhaps if I am astride and not perched on her side like a decoration, I can coax some life back into her.'

'Certainly not!' It was not quite the shout he had released during their wedding, but it was bad enough.

She sighed. 'Very well, then. If you insist, I shall ride like an old woman, on an old woman.' She glanced at him as she was lifted up into the saddle and muttered, 'Beside an old woman as well.' Then, she gave her horse a quick nudge to pull in front of him.

'What did you say?'

'Nothing, my dear.' She turned back to him, offering a dim-witted and adoring smile, then cantered towards the street.

He caught up to her easily, offering a polite dip of his head to the ladies crossing in front of them as they turned into traffic. They looked up at him and giggled before hurrying on. From each woman they passed as they rode, he received more simpering and blushes, and she saw obvious looks of envy at her marital success.

George could not deny he made an attractive companion. It was a shame that she did not share in the public enthusiasm for the man. As she glanced back at him, she could see his look of annoyance that she'd outpaced him again. In her opinion, he could have saved himself the irritation if he had been willing to keep a reasonable pace. She mentally crossed off the first day in the duration of the truce. It was going to be a long month.

He was smiling at her as if it caused him physical pain to do so. 'Perhaps you should let me lead. The traffic near Hyde Park can be unnerving.'

'Are you speaking to me, or the horse?' she said and gave a gentle shift of the reins to increase the distance. 'I assure you, a few people on the street and the odd carriage is in no way alarming.'

He spurred to catch up. 'Then perhaps you should allow me to lead as a sign of respect,' he suggested.

She nudged her horse to be one step ahead of his. 'Perhaps, if you were to go faster, we would be walking side by side.'

'I have no intention of racing through the streets to get to the park,' he countered.

'Racing?' It took all her restraint not to show him what a race actually looked like. 'I doubt that would be possible with this poor beast. If we were to trade mounts, you could best me with a display of superior horsemanship and not just by being larger and louder.'

'I am not louder.' Even as he'd said the words, his volume had increased. He paused to regain control of himself before speaking. 'And I say again, there is no reason to rush, nor do we need to make a simple ride into a contest of wills.'

'If you mean to dominate me in every small detail of my life, then you can expect many more such contests,' she said, deliberately spurring her horse to a trot.

He increased his pace to match hers, riding at her side, as she suggested. 'Do not think, because I yield to you now, that I intend to let you set the pace of our marriage for me.'

They had arrived at Hyde Park already and were turning onto Rotten Row. Even she had to admit that the middle of a crowd of gossipy riders was no place to continue the argument, so she gave him the same insincere smile he was giving her. 'If I wish to set a faster pace for our partnership, it is only because I want it to be over as soon as possible.' Then she turned deliberately away to admire the carriage that had just passed them.

It was smartest curricle she had ever seen. Balanced high on its two large wheels, it was a hundred times more interesting than the sensible barouche that had delivered them to the town house ycstcrday. She looked up to see a familiar face smiling down from the driver's seat. 'Mr Gregory?'

She shouldn't have used such a questioning tone. There was no mistaking Oliver Gregory for anyone but who he was. His dark skin and dazzling white smile had set maidens' hearts fluttering all over London. But like all the rest of the mothers, Marietta had forbidden her to make his acquaintance.

He is not our sort.

By that, George had assumed she'd been referring to his being Indian. But really, he was only half so. Since it had not diminished his manners and had improved his looks, it was a strange thing to bother about.

'Mrs Challenger.' He gave a respectful bow of his head and another especially pleased smile. Then he grinned past her, at his friend. ''Lo, Fred. Out and about already?'

Mr Challenger shrugged and smiled back, relaxing. 'Satisfying the curiosity of the *ton*.'

'But your bride is curious as well, I see.' He had noticed her interest in his carriage.

'Yellow wheels,' she said in awe, reaching out to touch the rim that stood even taller than her horse.

'I would settle for nothing less,' Mr Gregory said.

'And your horses are a right pair of steppers, aren't they?'

He nodded. 'The best I could find at Tattersall's. I outbid the Regent himself for them.'

Perhaps it was an exaggeration. But they were the sort of cattle fit for royalty. She grinned. 'How fast do you think they will go?'

'I have been to Croydon and back in less than two hours.'

Her eyes widened. 'I would love to take them out some day.'

He laughed. 'You?'

'Just a run down the coach road. No more than a couple of miles.'

Beside her, Mr Challenger cleared his throat. 'Perhaps, when we retire to Richmond in July, I will buy you a pony cart. Once you have learned to manage that, we will see about a larger carriage.'

George turned to look at him, rolling her

eyes. 'Or you could get me a milk wagon pulled by dogs.' She had been having such a good time talking to Mr Gregory that she had almost forgotten she was married. Leave it to Frederick Challenger to ruin everything. 'I have been driving my father's gig in the country since I was twelve. He says I am as good as a boy with the ribbons.' Or at least he had until he had married Marietta and taken no more notice of anything she had done.

'Do you seriously think you can handle a curricle?' Mr Gregory said with admiration of his own.

'Oliver.'

The signal word of warning from Mr Challenger put him on his guard again and he shook his head in regret. But he was looking at her with speculation, as if wondering just what she might be capable of if she could slip the tight leash Mr Challenger wanted to put on her. 'Fred will have my hide if anything happens to you.'

She seriously doubted it. She leaned forward and said in a mock whisper that she was sure Mr Challenger could hear, 'He need not know. It will be our secret.'

'Georgiana!' This time she was the one to receive the warning.

For a moment, she debated continuing to argue, then thought the better of it. While it did not matter to her what Mr Challenger thought, she did not think it fair to trap the charming Mr Gregory in the middle of their quarrel. She turned to her husband and smiled. 'Yes, Frederick. I will behave.'

He should have known better than to believe her. But at the sound of his Christian name, his look of suspicion softened to confusion. Then he snapped back to being his usual difficult self. 'We will discuss the wisdom of your carriage driving when we are home. At the moment, I wish to speak to Mr Gregory. It concerns the club.' The look he gave her now indicated that they wished for privacy. He pointed down the path. 'I see your stepmother just ahead. She will, no doubt, wish to speak to you.'

'No doubt,' George snapped, before remembering that she was supposed to be agreeable. Then she turned her horse and set off down the path at a walk so slow that even Mr Challenger could have kept pace with it. Why, of all people, did she have to talk to Marietta?

She had written a letter to Father after breakfast, to assure him that she was well. She had included a few gentle hints about her eagerness to see him soon. It was not like gentlemen to make social calls in the morning the way ladies did. But perhaps he might find a few minutes on his way to and from Westminster to stop for a cup of tea and admire his daughter's new home.

But she had assumed, since she was marrying and leaving his house for ever, that the Lord would give her at least one day's respite from the woman who had despised her since she was twelve. She already had to deal with the critical opinions of Mr Challenger. Was it so much to ask that only one person hate her at a time?

Nor did she need to be reminded again that her taste in clothing did not compare to the fashionable set in London. Her husband was wearing a bottle-green coat and immaculate buff britches. His friend, Mr Gregory, wore a red coat and his linen was white as snow. Marietta's habit was as blue as a summer sky, topped with a high, plumed hat. She was also sitting aside the chestnut gelding that George had been riding less than a week ago.

And George was riding a nag and wearing brown twill. Again. Until now, she had been perfectly satisfied with her habit. It was new this Season, but was far more suitable for a rough country gallop than the parade that Londoners seemed to enjoy. On the sad mare that Challenger had chosen for her, she felt dowdy and out of sorts. Even the liveried groom that rode one pace behind her stepmother dressed in the Grinsted colours of blue and gold was more elegantly attired than she was.

Her husband had said nothing about her choice of clothing when they'd left the house. Perhaps he was waiting until they returned home to inform her that people had been staring at her for all the wrong reasons, when she'd been hoping that they would not notice her at all. If only the blandness of her dress could camouflage her, then maybe Marietta would ride on without noticing her. Or perhaps, now that they were not forced to share a household, her stepmother would simply cut her dead and pretend that they did not know each other.

Instead Marietta turned her horse to watch her approach and called, 'Georgiana!', welcoming her with an elegant wave of her hand as if,

after years of hatred, she was suddenly over-
joyed to see her.

George braced herself for the inevitable argument, before remembering Mr Challenger's
desire that they seem to be a loving couple.
For once, she agreed with him. To be anything
less than brilliantly happy with the match she
had made would give her stepmother one more
reason to gloat. 'Marietta!' She followed the
greeting with her most brilliant smile.

Her stepmother leaned forward, kissing the
air in her direction, as if only the inconvenience of the horses kept her from offering a
warm, physical greeting. 'It is such a surprise
to see you out and about. And so early.'

'It is nearly five,' George replied. 'The perfect time for a ride.'

'But on the day after your wedding?' Marietta's eyes were wide with mocking amazement. 'I thought you would be staying at home
today.'

'Is there some rule that requires I stay in the
house?' George asked sweetly, half wondering
if it were true.

'Not a rule, exactly. But I would think, with
a husband as handsome as Frederick Chal-

lenger, a leisurely day at home would be preferable to riding...on a horse.'

George smiled again to hide her confusion, but gave no answer. What other kind of riding was there?

Now Marietta wore the satisfied smile of a cream-fed cat. 'Most happy brides would not leave their husband's side for weeks.'

'She has not.' Mr Challenger had ridden up to join them. His stallion stomped impatiently, but the man in the saddle was as suave and pleasant as she could have hoped. 'It was my suggestion that we come out together. It is a beautiful day and even newlyweds benefit from a brief exposure to sunshine.'

'And Georgiana is able to sit a horse,' Marietta said, as if that was in some way unusual.

'You know I can ride,' George said, surprised at the odd statement. 'And it is not at all difficult to sit the tired, grey mare that Mr Challenger has chosen me,' she added, giving her husband an overly toothy smile.

'It is, indeed, a very gentle horse,' he responded, not even looking at her. Instead, he had locked eyes with Marietta.

In response, her stepmother gave a small, knowing nod.

George frowned. It was clear that something had passed in the exchange that she had missed. But she would rather die than to admit her ignorance to either of them, so she smiled and nodded as if to confirm what her husband had said.

Marietta sighed, but not with the happy contentment that the news warranted. 'That is for the best, I suppose. And I assume you are enjoying your marriage?'

'Of course, we are,' Mr Challenger replied, his gaze never wavering. 'Is there a reason we should not be?'

Marietta arched her eyebrows in surprise. 'Just a few weeks ago, Georgiana showed no interest in matrimony.' Perhaps Mr Challenger had been right about the need to prevent tattle. Marietta announced the truth with relish, as if she had come to the park for the purpose of telling everyone she knew that their wedding had been some sort of sham.

'She was not interested in other men because she had already met me,' Mr Challenger said with such insufferable confidence that George would have corrected him, had he been speaking to anyone else in the world.

Marietta persisted. 'But before your offer, Georgiana made no effort to hide her dislike of you. In fact, she was most adamant that she would not so much as speak to you, much less dance with you.'

'Marietta.' George redoubled her smile and bit back the response she longed to give. Even if it was true, it was rude to throw the facts in Mr Challenger's face. She had left home, just as her stepmother had wanted, and allowed the woman to win the battle for Father's whole attention. There was no reason to continue to torment her.

'Her obvious animosity towards me shows what a clever actress she is,' her husband said, turning to George with a doting smile. 'She was worried that, should our mutual affection become common knowledge, you would disapprove.'

'Disapprove of an earl's son?' Marietta replied, suspicious.

'A second son,' Mr Challenger reminded her. 'I am sure Georgiana could have aimed much higher. She is both a wit and a beauty.'

Apparently, he was a good actor as well. He'd given the compliment with such sincerity that George could not help but blush with pleasure. 'You are too kind, my dear. And a title is nothing compared to good character and good looks.' Then she smiled, more for herself than either of them, for she had managed to deliver a compliment without a single lie in it.

'But you might have given some indication of your plans. This marriage was so very sudden.'

'You said it was time that I was out of the house,' George countered.

'But Mr Challenger's offer was a surprise, all the same,' Marietta said. 'After all, you did have an understanding with Sir Nash.'

'There was no understanding.' George could feel her limited patience dwindle to nothing.

Marietta sighed as if the news pained her. 'He has gone from town, you know.'

'Good riddance.' Georgiana made no effort to conceal her feelings. If her stepmother wished to goad her to argument, then let it happen. She could not stand Nash Bowles and should not have to pretend to do so, just to keep the peace. Mr Challenger already thought her a foolish child. A tantrum in public would only cement his bad opinion of her, but it could not be helped.

'What a horrible thing for you to say.' Marietta said with a moue of displeasure. 'He was never anything but kind to you and he left London the minute he heard of your engagement. I am sure his heart was broken by the news.'

Before she could reply, Mr Challenger spoke. 'Then we will do our best to dispel the rumours already spreading about his departure.'

'Rumours?' Marietta prided herself on knowing all that was worth knowing in London. But by the look on her face, there was some story she had not heard.

Mr Challenger gave a self-conscious laugh. 'My friend, Mr Gregory, said when last he saw your cousin, it was not his heart that had been broken.' Her husband laid a finger at the side of his nose to indicate the location that had been damaged. 'He was involved in a dispute at the Murder of Crows, the other night. That is a gaming hell in Mayfair,' he added for George. 'He was involved in a physical altercation that had something to do with an unpaid debt of his and markers that had not been honoured. They are not the most charitable people there, I fear. It is a very unsavoury place.'

Marietta's eyes narrowed. 'I am sure it is nothing more than a coincidence.'

'Of course,' Mr Challenger agreed. 'I am simply repeating what I have heard. I would never share the tale about town. We both know how disturbing it is to spread harmful gossip.' As they had when making cryptic comments about her horse, her husband and stepmother were talking past her, again. But this exchange was easier to understand. He was warning Marietta to keep her mouth closed about other people's families if she did not want tales told about hers.

'Of course,' Marietta replied, then turned back to Georgiana. 'I will not delay you further. I am sure you have places to be.' Then she turned her horse and trotted away from them.

'Send Father my love,' George called to the woman's retreating back, wondering if the message would be relayed. Perhaps, if he knew she was thinking of him, he would at least write to her so she might know that she had not been forgotten after her departure.

'It appears that you were right in your assumption that Bowles wanted more from you than the obvious.' Mr Challenger spoke with no preamble, startling her.

She turned to stare at him, surprised to find that he was addressing her without a trace of sarcasm. 'The obvious?'

'Your person,' he said, giving her an appraising look. 'Surely you knew I was not exaggerating when I remarked on your beauty just now.'

She had not thought his praise was an exaggeration so much as an outright lie. Now, the repeat of it caught her unprepared. 'Th-thank you.' The comment was hardly worth stuttering over. She knew that she was pretty and was modest enough not to dwell on the fact. But she had not thought he'd noticed. Then, she remembered their kiss.

He went on, unmoved. 'It appears he wanted your inheritance, as well. Just as you thought,' he said. 'An impending marriage to an heiress was the only thing keeping the debt collectors at bay.'

'Then I am doubly glad to have disappointed him,' George said with an evil grin. 'If ever a man deserved a good thrashing, it was Sir Nash Bowles.'

'It is most unladylike for you to say so,' he said with no trace of his usual frown. 'But I think a lapse in decorum can be forgiven, just this once.'

Chapter Nine

All in all, Fred considered it a successful day. They had ridden. He had written letters in the late afternoon and she had gone shopping on Bond Street, like all the other females in London. Dinner had been quiet, but cordial. When he had left the house at eleven, his wife had already retired for the evening behind her locked bedroom door. But tonight, it had not been slammed, nor had flowers or any other objects been thrown at his person.

Now, he sat in his favourite leather armchair in the owners' suite at Vitium et Virtus, enjoying an excellent brandy and contemplating their meeting with his wife's stepmother. He had not liked Marietta Knight, even before he had married Georgiana. She always seemed to be sticking her nose where it didn't belong, gathering and sharing gossip. Far too often, the stories she had spread involved the Challenger family.

Thus, he had taken pains to avoid her and her stepdaughter. But he had begun to wonder if he had been fair in associating Georgiana with the actions of Lady Grimsted.

On their meeting in Hyde Park she had proved what an odious woman she actually was. What sort of mother quizzed her daughter in such detail about the activities of the wedding night? He had not sensed the curiosity to be prurient, so much as it was a test to prove the new bride was either still ignorant of the marital act, or miserable in her choice of partners. It was as if Marietta Knight had been eager to see her daughter unhappy.

Georgiana was still every bit as naïve as she had been when she had got herself into the muddle that had required his proposal. She'd had no idea what the woman was asking her about. It was fortunate that he had been there to guide the conversation. Even more so that he had rented such a tame mare so he might spin the choice to make it seem protective of his wife's intimate person, as opposed to the display of general caution he had intended.

Lady Grimsted's continued obsession with

Bowles spoke volumes as well. The man was family and deserved some support. But she'd kept hammering away at a union that was impossible now that George had married. She seemed to want Georgiana to argue with her, just to put the girl in a bad light. She had behaved the same way before the wedding, causing a needless delay and then blaming it on the bride.

It made him wonder how many of the faults he had found with the girl before their marriage were the result of her stepmother's dislike of her. He knew from experience how continual rebellion against family could change the shape of one's character until one became the very thing one abhorred in others. Before the army, he'd very nearly become the worst sinner in the family. And yet, he'd never stopped blaming the others for their scandalous reputation.

'Challenger!' Oliver appeared in the doorway and took the briefest stop at the side table to fill a glass before cuffing the back of Fred's head as he had done when they were in school together. The gesture was intended as one of *bon ami*, but tonight it was delivered with such enthusiasm that it nearly knocked the glass from Fred's hand.

'Gregory?' He raised his glass in a toast of greeting, before draining it and setting it aside.

'I must right a wrong.' Oliver pulled a chair up beside him and sipped his own drink. 'I offered you congratulations at your wedding and again today. But I fear they were half-hearted.'

'In what way?' He could not remember any hesitation on the part of his friends. Perhaps because he was too absorbed in his own feelings about the event.

'Your marriage was so very sudden,' Oliver said, with a shake of his head. 'You, of all people, would know your own mind and think before making such a momentous decision. But I feared…'

'Me, of all people?' Fred raised an eyebrow.

'Well…' Oliver shrugged and pointed to the bottle and Fred poured him another class. 'You have always been conscious of society's opinion of you.'

'Too conscious, you usually say,' Fred reminded him.

'There is no pleasing the world,' Oliver said. 'Once it has formed a negative opinion, it will not see reason. I see no point in trying to change its collective mind, especially when conformity to the norm interferes with my pleasure.'

Fred nodded in sympathy. Because of his Indian blood, many people turned their back on his friend before they'd even met him. Yet, the Challenger family was accepted into the best homes, no matter what awful thing they did. There was no fairness in it. 'I do not behave as I do just to please society,' he replied. 'Having seen the alternative, I prefer order and moderation.'

'In public, at least,' Oliver said, glancing towards the main rooms where naked women posed on daises for the admiration of the guests. 'I can remember many nights here at the club where moderation was the last thing you would have suggested.'

'Not in quite some time.' It had taken just one particularly horrible incident to sour him on the games they'd played at Vitium et Virtus. Now, he could walk past a line of dancers wearing little more than grease paint and feathers and think of nothing more scandalous than his desire to hole up in the office with a book and a bottle. But he had never shared his reason for drawing away from the entertainment with his friend and did not plan to do so tonight.

Instead, he smiled. 'Perhaps, I am just getting too old to be dancing drunk on top of the tables.'

'And Jake is a duke now and far too proper,' Oliver mocked. 'The pair of you are younger than me...'

'Barely,' Fred reminded him.

'And yet, lately you act like old ladies. If I am to go to Paris and speak to the fellows at Club Plaisirs Nocturnes about new entertainments for this place only to have the pair of you sell your shares and bow out of management, I would rather not make the trip.'

Though they had been close since childhood, they were grown men with responsibilities. Change was inevitable. Perhaps Oliver felt it more keenly and was worried about the loss of his old friends. 'Do not fear on that account,' Frederick said, to set his mind at rest. 'I am still as committed as ever to see the place run smoothly.'

'So that others might have fun where you refuse to.' Oliver shook his head in disgust. 'What will your wife say to the time you spend, here? Does she not fear you will be tempted?'

'What can she say?' Frederick said. If she uttered a word, other than profound thanks for getting her out of the mess she'd made, he had no wish to hear it. 'I have no intention of allowing her to rule my life and set my schedule.'

'But if she grows bored...' Oliver said, giving him a significant look.

'Then she can take up needlework, or whatever it is that women do when their husbands are not at home,' Fred finished.

Oliver was shaking his head again. 'Did you receive a blow to the head in battle that has knocked all the sense of out of you? Or do you really know so little about women, after all this time?' He pointed towards the ceiling. 'The bedrooms above us are full of bored wives and they are not painting watercolours. When their husbands are not home, they come here to find other men, or sometimes other women.'

'But Georgiana is not like that,' he said. 'She is still an innocent.'

Oliver raised his eyebrows in surprise.

'Mostly innocent,' Fred corrected. 'Certainly too naïve to go behind my back to spite me.'

'Because you have been married for a day and

a half,' Oliver finished, then grinned. 'And yet, she has already found a way to get around you.'

'She did what?' Fred leaned forward in his chair.

'As I said before, my well-wishes were tepid at the ceremony, for I could not see what you would want with a milk-and-water miss. But now that I have got to know her better, I totally understand the attraction.'

'You do.' If he had not been honest enough to admit to his own friends the reason he was marrying, he had expected they would form some conclusion on their own. But did they seriously believe that it was a love match?

'Indeed. If I were in any way inclined to marry, I might have snapped her up myself.' Then he held up a hand to dismiss the idea, hurriedly pouring himself another drink. 'Not that you need have any worries about my interference in your marriage. But knowing her as you do, you should realise that she is far too spirited to sit at home alone waiting for you to return.'

'You think so, do you?' Fred said, annoyed. The idea had not entered his head at all until Oliver had put it there.

'A few more exploits like the one today and

you will be the envy of every man in London. The girl is magnificent, Challenger.' Oliver's eyes were wide with admiration, as was the grin on his face.

'Georgiana?' Fred's eyes narrowed as he poured another glass of brandy for himself, drinking deeply. 'She is pretty, of course...' Which was quite understating the case. From the first moment he'd seen her, he had decided to avoid her lest her beauty blind him towards her quite obvious faults. But what had his friend meant by 'exploits'?

Oliver shook his head. 'I will not deny that she is a looker,' his friend agreed. 'I am not blind, you know. But even though she claimed she could drive, I did not think she'd be such a dab hand with a whip.'

'A what?'

'A skilled driver,' Oliver repeated. 'This afternoon...'

'She was shopping this afternoon,' Fred said.

'Not for long,' Oliver said. 'She drove my curricle back from Hounslow Heath,' he continued, oblivious to Fred's shock.

'Drove, or raced?' The road he was describing sounded like the Hounslow Road towards

Colnbrook, a notorious straight that young men used to test the wind of their horses.

'She tracked me down in Bond Street,' Oliver admitted. 'She was burdened with packages, so I offered her a ride back to your town house, and the next thing I knew...'

'You gave her the reins,' Fred said, shaking his head.

'She bet me a guinea,' Oliver added helplessly.

'Oh. Well, then...' he said, sarcastically. But Oliver could hardly be blamed. The girl was a corrupting influence on the best of men. 'What were you thinking? She might have broken her neck. Then you could have taken your winnings from my dead wife's reticule and bought me a funeral wreath for the front door.'

This was met by an embarrassed silence.

'I trust you put her in her place,' Fred said.

Oliver shrugged.

'You did not let her beat you?' There was such a thing as carrying chivalry too far, especially when it involved a friend's wife.

'I did not let her do anything,' Oliver said sheepishly. 'I drove out at a brisk pace. Not as fast as I might have, of course. I did not want to frighten the girl.'

'Of course not,' Fred agreed.

'But fast enough to take the devil out of the horses and cause her to lose her bonnet.'

'And I suppose she cried over that,' Fred said, hoping.

'Not a tear. She was too busy timing me with her little gold watch to notice. When we reached the mile marker, she held out her hands for the reins, turned the carriage like she'd been driving it for years and—' Oliver clapped his hands '—we were off without giving the horses a chance to take a second breath.'

'And she beat you,' Fred said again.

'I would have shown no mercy at all if I'd known she could drive like a demon.' Oliver paused, as if suddenly remembering that this was not some fellow they both knew, but a woman. 'A very attractive demon, of course,' he finished.

'Attractive?' Fred repeated in a dark tone to remind that she was not just some girl, but the woman who had just become his wife.

'Um, yes,' Oliver said cautiously. 'But also very ladylike, I am sure. She said she was taking her winnings to Bond Street to buy a new hat, since I had ruined hers.' He grinned at the memory. 'She is very like you were, at her age.'

'When I was her age, I was still at Oxford.' And many of the stories from school still made him wince in embarrassment.

'Exactly. And a young hellion, just as we all were.' Oliver smiled fondly at the memory. 'I had no idea that young ladies could have the same daring streak in them. But apparently, some do.'

'Then they should have it trained out of them,' Fred said firmly.

'I am sure there is no harm in it,' Oliver said, attempting to bury a situation that he had enabled. 'As long as you are not serious in thinking she will stay by the hearth fire while you neglect her.'

'I have no intention of neglecting her,' he said. The negligence would be mutual. It was hardly a mistake if he was doing exactly what she wanted by leaving her alone.

'That is good to hear,' Oliver said. 'Whether you realise it or not, you married that girl to fill the void in your spirit that we have all noticed since you returned from fighting Napoleon.'

'There is such a thing as too much spirit,' Fred said darkly. 'What will the world think if it finds that after barely a day of marriage she is cavorting with one of my oldest friends?'

'Cavorting?' At this, Oliver laughed. 'Is that all you are worried about? I thought you were concerned about the danger of driving breakneck in an open carriage and the possibility that we could have upset and been injured or killed. But if it is our cavorting you are worried about…'

What was he saying? He was supposed to be newly married and in love. If not besotted, he should at least care enough about his wife to worry more about her safety than his own pride. 'Of course,' he corrected. 'I am worried for her safety.'

'And, *of course*, you are jealous,' Oliver agreed, with another laugh. 'Jealous that I will suddenly forget two decades of friendship and steal your bride. You are being ridiculous, but I forgive you for it. Men in love seldom think with the head on their shoulders.'

So his friend thought he was ruled by lust. They must be better actors than he had thought, if even those closest to him were seeing signs of affection between them. 'I apologise. It is just as you say. I am being ridiculous.'

Oliver nodded. 'It is understandable. As I

said before, Challenger, what a woman.' He was still smiling in admiration, as if Fred had somehow won first place, even though he had not been racing.

Chapter Ten

When George came down to the breakfast room the next morning, Mr Challenger was there to greet her with his usual disapproving expression.

'Good morning, Husband,' she said, smiling brightly. Then, for the benefit of the footman, she went to his side and gave him a kiss upon the cheek before taking her seat. When she glanced back at him while reaching for the eggs it was clear that the gesture had affected him. He was still frowning, but his cheeks had gone pink and it looked as though he had forgotten what it was he meant to say.

At last, he settled on, 'Good morning, Georgiana.'

Silence fell, again. She sipped her tea.

'Did you enjoy your shopping trip yesterday?' He would not have asked if he did not know the truth. She smiled sweetly. 'Yes. Very much so. I bought a new bonnet.'

'To replace the one you lost while carriage racing on the Hounslow Road,' he finished, taking a slice of toast from the rack and reaching for the butter. 'Did you not listen to a word I said, on the night we married?'

She touched a finger to her chin, pretending to think. 'I believe you wished me to be frugal. Since I got the money for the hat off Mr Gregory, it cost you nothing.'

The bread in his hand crumbled under the pressure of his knife and he tossed it uneaten on his plate. 'I also told you to avoid making a public spectacle of yourself.'

'A public spectacle?' She laughed. 'It was only a mile down the road and back.'

'In the company of a man who is not your husband,' he reminded her.

'A good friend of yours. Surely...'

'And betting.'

'One small wager,' she said. 'Which I won.'

'The amount is not the point,' Mr Challenger said. 'The point is that I forbade you from driving...'

'Not exactly,' she said. 'You threatened me with a pony cart.'

'I do not threaten,' he said.

It was not really a threat to be so over-protective. He might have been trying, in his own misguided way, to be kind. He had followed it by defending her against Marictta. For the first time in ages, someone had taken her side in an argument. Despite how much he annoyed her, she had wanted to kiss him in gratitude.

And then, on the ride back to the house, he had told her of his plans to abandon her for the evening to go to his stupid club.

An hour later, she had been tearing down the road toward Colnbrook with the wind in her hair and her husband's friend swearing on the driver's seat beside her.

'You do not threaten?' She smiled and took a sip of tea. 'Well, neither do I. I said I had no intention of following the ridiculous strictures you placed on me. And I meant it.'

She waited for his response. He did not seem like the sort of man who would strike a woman. But what could he do to her, short of lock her in her room? She almost hoped he would try, so she might test the strength of the drainpipe outside her bedroom window.

'Then I will renege on my part of the bargain,' he said, smiling over his coffee cup.

'And what might that bargain be?' she asked, feeling the first hint of worry.

He set down his cup and stood, walking over to stand behind her chair, resting his hands on the back, so she could feel the heat of his fingers through the back of her gown. He bent down until his lips were touching her ear. Then he whispered in a voice so soft that the footman at the door would not hear a word. 'You wish to live apart? If you do not obey me, it will never happen. You will never be rid of me, until death us do part, just as the bishop said. We will be together, night and day. We will live in the same house. We will sleep in the same bed.'

'You would not dare,' she whispered back. 'I would not...' She turned her head to whisper back into his face. And this time she was the one who forgot how to speak. Their lips were less than an inch from each other, so close that she could smell the coffee on his breath.

When he kissed her, it was more gentle than their last kiss had been, as if it was nothing more than his answer to the morning greeting she had just given him. His hands were on her shoulders, kneading the muscles until she was near to purring with pleasure. She could not help herself. She kissed him back, eager for more.

Then he kissed his way back to her ear, nibbling the lobe before whispering again, in a calm, unemotional tone, 'If you do not obey me by choice, I have the power to make you beg to do exactly what I want. Do not forget it.'

Then he stood up and gave her an avuncular pat on the back. 'Have a good time on Bond Street, my sweet. And be sure that shopping is all you do today.'

The man was insufferable. She had known it from the first moment they'd met. But then, she had not seen the worst of him. At first, she had hated him without reservation. Now, that hatred was mingled with confusion. When she'd agreed to the marriage, she'd had no idea that his kisses could make her act against her better judgement.

When he was not kissing her, she was as resolved as ever to go where she pleased and do as she pleased. But with one touch of his lips, she could imagine nothing more pleasurable than total compliance to whatever he suggested. And while he was not totally unmoved by her presence, she saw no sign that receiving a kiss from her could similarly move him to become more reasonable.

But knowledge of the fact did nothing to help her decide how to spend the day in a way that did not annoy him or bore herself. She wrote a brief note to her father to tell him of the carriage race, then tore it up before sending it. At one time, he'd have thought it the most amusing thing in the world. But perhaps now he would disapprove, just as her husband did. It might create an even greater wedge between them. In the end, she wrote a whole page of boring nonsense that even Marietta could not object to and closed with another invitation to tea.

After such a bland missive, it seemed only natural to spend the rest of the day behaving in the conventional manner that her husband expected. She spoke with the housekeeper about the week's menus, spent some time familiarising herself with the household accounts, then dressed to go out. She made her first official social call: a visit to the home of her husband's brother to see her sister-in-law, Caroline. Between them, they agreed to take his younger sisters shopping that afternoon.

He could not possibly object to her making

nice with his family. Though she'd had no luck with her own, it was her duty to make an attempt with his. A success with the Challengers might prove to him that she was not as difficult as he claimed.

At least she could be less contrary than her husband himself. On their wedding day, he'd made little effort to encourage a friendship between her and the ladies of the family, treating them every bit as rudely as he had her. Now that they'd spoken, she found Caroline to be quite charming and just as eager to accept her friendship as she was to offer it.

Neither was it hard to gain the approval of the younger sisters. On their shopping trip, the three girls occupying the carriage seat opposite her were lovely and well mannered, so she told them so. In response, they giggled. Judging by their behaviour at the wedding, it was their answer of choice for many situations.

'Do not be tiresome, girls. If your incessant chatter gives me a megrim I will take you home immediately.' Caroline, Viscountess Linholm, might have experience with the girls, but she had far less patience.

The eldest of the three was barely fourteen. George remembered the age well and how hard it was to balance the desire to be a grown up with the fact that ladylike behaviour was boring. When the novelty of hair ribbons and bonbons wore off, George did a thing she had always wished someone would do for her.

She took them to a pet store. There she bought them a shiny black bird that the store owner assured them could be trained to speak. It already had a vocabulary of some sort, though as far as George knew, it was mostly gibberish. After some discussion, it was decided that he would be named Pootah, after one of the sounds he kept repeating.

Once they had the bird to occupy them, they did not mind being sent home so the ladies could continue to shop. As the carriage rolled down the street and away from her, George saw them passing the cage back and forth between them, offering Pootah bits of biscuit and trying to coax him into saying hello.

'Now that those annoying children are gone, the real fun can begin,' Caroline said, taking George gently by the shoulders and casting a sidelong look down at her day dress. 'The first thing we must do is to get you to my modiste.' Though she smiled as she said it and was nowhere near as critical as Marietta, it was plain that she found fault with George's clothing.

George glanced down at it herself to see if there was something obviously wrong. 'I hardly think it necessary. I bought a new wardrobe at the beginning of the Season.'

'For your come-out,' Caroline replied with a shake of her head. 'Those dresses were all well and good for a green virgin. But you are married now.'

And the dresses still suited her. She was almost as green and definitely as virginal as she had been a couple of days ago. The few kisses she'd exchanged with Mr Challenger so far put her on par with some of the other girls she had befriended who had been able to dodge their chaperones long enough to experiment with such things.

If her husband did not want the world to see her as an innocent, she had best not look like one. 'I am married,' George admitted cautiously. 'But I do not know if Mr Challenger wishes for me to spend all of his money at the dressmaker.'

'How else would he want you to spend it?' Caroline replied. 'And even if you are right about his opinion, you must not take Frederick's word as law. The whole family knows that he is a miser and a fussbudget. If he is allowed to, he will see you in rags and think it good value.'

But he was her husband, at least for the month, and George felt required to defend him, though she had no real desire to do so. 'He has been most generous with me thus far. And I would hardly call him a fussbudget.' Stick in the mud? Joyless authoritarian? There were any number of more accurate phrases, none of which she desired to share with Caroline on their first meeting.

'All the same, you cannot go out with him in the modest attire of a girl. You are a lady now. People will expect elegance.'

This was a conundrum. For when she looked at the Viscountess's wardrobe she could not say that she actually liked it. It was expensive, of course. And very *au courant*. Marietta had often said, with guarded admiration, that the woman never wore the same gown more than once. Even so, George doubted that many of the styles she had seen so far would suit her. She did not wish to wear a cap in the house just because she was married. She certainly did not want one like the starched organza confection favoured by Caroline when she'd called upon her. Nor did she want ballgowns that were cut so low one was in danger of falling out of them if one sneezed.

But perhaps it was not about what she wanted at all. It was clear that Mr Challenger did not like her as she was. She had said she would not change. If she could dress the part of a good wife when they were together, she might not have to alter anything else about herself.

The choice of gowns had been one of the chief battles between her and Marietta. If her new sister-in-law did not like her clothing either, maybe it was time to admit that she might be wrong on the subject. 'Perhaps I do need some help choosing a fashion that suits me,' George said hesitantly. 'We are attending a ball this evening hosted by Frederick's friend, the Duke of Westmoor. I do want to look my best for it and would be most happy for you to advise me.'

'Excellent!' the woman responded, clapping her hands in approval. 'You will not be sorry that you have put yourself in my hands.

This proved false almost immediately.

It was four in the afternoon, well past the

time George liked to be sitting down to tea. And yet the Viscountess was still calling for more silks.

'The stripes next. With tassels of gold,' Caroline announced, helping herself to the sweetmeats displayed on the gold ormolu table in the corner of the fitting room. The dressmaker's assistant scurried for the back room to get more fabric.

George's stomach growled in response. She lowered her arms for a moment to shake the numbness from them and received a disapproving sniff from the modiste who was trying to adjust the armhole of the sample gown so it might be possible to dance without ripping out a seam.

Caroline's choices so far had been less outrageous than she'd feared. The current dress— a grass-green silk with gold-embroidered hem—was quite pretty, though shockingly low-cut. But if she stood for stripes and tassels, she would end up looking like the ottoman Caroline was perched on. 'Do we not have enough gowns already?' she asked.

'For evening, perhaps,' the Viscountess said. 'But what of days and mornings? And you have no fans or gloves as yet.'

George had a drawer full of white gloves that would go with the dresses she had bought and nearly as many fans. Since her plan was to leave London as soon as she was able, her current day clothes would do nicely. They were well made, comfortable, and never seen by neighbours in the country.

Today, she must find another method to dissuade her new friend that did not display her disappointing lack of interest in fashion plates. She blinked and smiled sweetly at the Viscountess. 'If we buy everything today, we will have nothing to shop for next week.'

'How true,' the Viscountess agreed. 'Perhaps the rest of the wardrobe can wait.'

'Wonderful.' George replied. 'And now, we can go for tea.'

'But tea shops are so stuffy. Fit only for girls and old ladies,' Caroline said. 'I would prefer something more filling. A meal at Steven's Hotel would do nicely.'

'Is it really necessary to go there without our husbands? Surely we will call attention.' While she did not wish to follow Mr Challenger's silly rules, neither did she want to flout convention just to spite him. Did ladies dine at hotels unescorted? She had heard Steven's was a gathering place for gentleman and former officers. If she was seen there by a member of her husband's old regiment, what would Mr Challenger say in response?

'Of course we will call attention, my dear,' The Viscountess replied with a wave of her scented handkerchief. 'That is the object of this whole endeavour. If we did not wish to be noticed, why else would we have left the house at all?'

George went straight to her room, when she returned home, not wanting to risk even a brief meeting with her husband. If he was to ask how she had spent her afternoon, she did not want to blurt out that it had ended in eating oysters and drinking champagne with half the Horse Guard.

She closed the door, locking it behind her, relieved that her maid was already in the room. 'Has a new ball gown arrived for me, Polly?'

'Yes, madam.' The girl grinned. 'And a fine thing it is.'

'I am glad you like it,' George replied, no longer sure what she thought about the dress, the Viscountess, or anything else. 'There will be a large number of them just as nice arriving in the next few days. When they come, you are to take up the bodices by at least an inch. I will not be seen in them unless you can manage to return some scrap of decency to the necklines. It is either that, or send them back unworn.' She sighed. 'But I expect it is too late for that already, if they have been fit for me. Lord knows what a row we will have when Mr Challenger sees the bills.' She had assumed the only instruction she might be capable of following was the avoidance of needless extravagance, but she had failed again. The mere thought of what she'd spent made her want to faint.

'Perhaps, if you model them for your husband before I alter them, he will not mind the price so very much.' By the sly tone in the maid's voice, she was expecting George to coax her way out of trouble with her non-existent feminine wiles.

If it saved her one evening's grief, it was worth trying. 'Very well,' she said with a shrug. 'Leave tonight's gown as it is. I doubt it will make matters worse than they already are.'

Chapter Eleven

The ball held in their honour by Jake Huntington was to be their first public appearance as a married couple and Fred wanted nothing less than perfection. It had been some months since Jake had been elevated to his father's title, but until now there had been no sign that he was ready to come out of his mourning and entertain. The Westmoor home had been shut tight against visitors for the whole of the Season, much to the disappointment of mothers with marriable daughters. A young bachelor duke was a precious commodity and his refusal to put away his blacks and secure the succession with marriage was considered not so much respect for the dead as disrespect of the natural order.

He had decided to make an exception to celebrate his friend's wedding. Fred had not thought it necessary to sit Georgiana down and lecture her on the significance of this event. She'd seemed properly impressed by the invitation on thick paper embossed with the gold Westmoor crest. But this party was so much more important than a normal social event. Jake would have been horrified to think his profound grief and social isolation was already the topic of worried conversation by his friends. If this ball signified an end, it was truly a reason to rejoice.

Fred would not see it ruined by a foolish girl who was likely to make them both late just to spite him. She had returned from shopping at six in the evening, long past the point where he feared she was not coming back at all. He had been ready to call for the servants to search the streets when he'd heard a slam of the front door and she'd breezed past his study without a word of apology or explanation.

A footman had followed a short time later, carrying a huge stack of boxes that offered Fred assurance that she had actually gone to Bond Street and not cock-fighting or some other totally unacceptable activity. Instead, she had been behaving like a normal female, wasting time and money, too obsessed with parading about the town to notice the trouble she was causing.

She had best get such vanity out of her system while she could. She might weep like a lost soul when he sent her to the country at the end of the month. But he would not be swayed by tears. There was no need to gild a lily with ruffles and lace. A lack of continual flattery by town dandies would not diminish her natural beauty and might improve her character.

Or perhaps he was wrong about her. At nine, he was waiting in the foyer, prepared to scold her for tardiness, only to have her appear at the head of the stairs just as the clock began to strike the hour. His watch slipped from his fingers, forgotten.

Oliver had been right. She was magnificent. The style she'd chosen for the evening was more sophisticated than the simple gowns she seemed to favour. While white was always fashionable, the green silk she wore tonight would turn heads and leave no doubt why he had married her. What sane man could resist a goddess?

She'd reached the foot of the stairs now, curtsying before him and spreading her skirts with a hopeful smile as if waiting for his approval. Did she actually care for his opinion? Or was she so hungry for praise that she would take it from a man whose company she barely tolerated?

If it was a trap to bring him to his knees before her, then she had succeeded. When he looked at her, all he could manage was an approving nod. How long had it been since the sight of a woman had robbed him of the power of speech? If it had been like this on the first night they'd met, things might have ended differently.

Actually, they might have ended nearly the same. He'd have offered for her before the evening was out and badgered, flattered, and cajoled until she'd accepted him. They'd have been married. He would have lost mastery of his life and future, but he'd have thought it a small sacrifice to win her love.

He had to fight for a moment to remember that love had never been the object. To the *ton*, the appearance of it mattered far more than the actual emotion ever would. And tonight, for all intents and purposes, she was his. And she was perfect.

He frowned. On closer inspection, she was not and he was the one at fault for it. Her neck, her ears and even the tops of her dancing slippers were bare of ornament. Who but a fool would bring his bride out into the world without a single piece of jewellery? He had married her with a simple gold ring and not bothered with a wedding gift. He had behaved as if his presence was gift enough. Since she had not complained of the absence of jewellery, he had not bothered to give her so much as a hairpin.

'Wait!' He sprinted past her, up the stairs to his room, rooting in the back of a bureau drawer to find the jewel case he had all but forgotten. His mother had handed it to him, announcing it was his share of the unentailed property that had belonged to his grandmother.

At the time, he had suspected that what he was receiving had already been rejected by both Mother and Caroline as too far out of style to bother with. Surely there was something in it that might do until he could get to a jewellery store. He opened it, rummaging through the contents for a suitable gift.

It was a sad collection of unmated earbobs and necklaces that were missing stones. But coiled at the bottom, he found a long gold chain, with matching gold eardrops.

His mind flashed to that moment he had seen

her on the auction block with a braided ribbon holding her dress. As it had that night, the floor seemed to shift under him. The room grew hot and he was struck by a sudden desire to cancel the outing and stay home with his wife. It took a supreme mastery of will to remember that he had never wanted to marry and especially did not want the woman he had chosen.

Want was the wrong word. He definitely wanted her in the way he usually wanted a woman: naked and in his bed. But when she had accepted his proposal, she had not wanted him. He had assured himself that there were enough other women in the world to make up for the loss of a single wife. Tonight, he was not so sure.

Make her want you.

He had threatened to do it this morning. Judging by the response when he kissed her, it was in his power to do so. At the same time, he recognised that it was unwise. Acting on his desire would complicate matters. There would be other, less irritating women in his future. Women he could walk away from when he was bored with them. It was better to wait.

When he turned to exit his room, it was with a clear head. By the time he'd reached the ground floor where his puzzled wife awaited him, his blood was cool as well.

He held out the chain to her. 'A token of my affection.'

She arched an eyebrow and gave him a sceptical half-smile, but her eyes sparkled as they looked at the necklace he held. 'It is lovely. Thank you.' She bowed her head. 'Help me with it.'

He draped it over her. Even looping it twice, it still hung low, lying heavy between her perfect breasts. For a moment, he watched it there, fascinated.

'Are there drops for my ears as well?' She tapped a finger on his closed hand to make him release the earrings he held. Her touch was warm. He moved slowly, letting her finger stroke his skin as he turned his hand over and opened his fist to reveal the rest of her gift.

She smiled and scooped them up, affixing them to her ears. Then she turned to him. 'How do I look?'

'Satisfactory,' he muttered.

'Liar,' she said with a smile. Then she slipped her hand into the crook of his arm. 'Let us be off. If we are late, I will not take the blame for it.'

* * *

George had never been to a gathering so wonderful, much less one thrown especially for her. The ballroom of the Duke of West-moor's manor was packed with the cream of the *ton* all eager to congratulate Mrs Challenger and her handsome husband. There was but one conspicuous absence.

She'd mailed her father's invitation herself, enclosing it in her daily letter. She had even bit her lip and included Marietta, though the sight of that woman was likely to spoil the whole evening for her. But she'd received no answer, nor had either of them appeared this evening.

There was probably a logical explanation for their absence. They might have already gone to the country and missed the post. Or it could be what she feared most: a deliberate snub. She tried not to think about that. Even if it was true, she did not want to spoil the evening by focusing on such a negative possibility.

As she stood admiring the dancers, the Duke himself came to her side. 'So, my friend refuses to dance with his wife.'

For a moment, she could not manage anything other than a wide-mouthed stare at the man beside her. It was not, precisely, that she had never spoken to a duke before. Her father was a viscount, after all. He had, if not exactly friends, at least acquaintances in the peerage. But that was all they had been to her: men who her father had known, who had no time to be bothered with a girl her age.

Even though her husband had introduced them at the wedding and again tonight, she was still adjusting to the fact that a peer was to be considered a close family friend. 'I am sure he means no offence by it,' she said. 'He is most grateful for the honour you've bestowed on us by hosting a ball. But he does not like to dance.' At least, that was what he'd claimed when he'd refused to stand up for the first set.

The Duke, who'd known Mr Challenger far longer than she, seemed surprised by the statement. He gave a slight shift of his head to indicate her husband, who was standing on the other side of the room, giving her a dark look. 'And yet he lingers near the dance floor to watch your every move.'

'He is probably waiting for me to do something that disappoints him,' she said, before remembering that it was not polite to sound glum at a party, especially when one was talking with the host.

The Duke laughed. 'On the contrary, my dear, the fellow is mad with jealousy over all the attention you are getting.'

'I seriously doubt that, Your Grace.'

'Come now, Mrs Challenger,' he said, touching her arm. 'I stood up at your wedding. Surely that is cause for us to be familiar with each other. You must call me Jacob, as your husband does.'

'Thank you?' The response should not have come out as a question, for it made her look even more naïve than she actually was.

But the Duke gave her an encouraging smile in response. 'Thank you, Jacob.'

She smiled back, instantly relaxed. 'Thank you, Jacob. And please, call me George.'

'A masculine name for such a pretty girl,' he replied. 'But it shall be as you wish. George, do not be bothered by your husband's moods. We must give him time to get used to marriage. Though I did not take the time to say so at your wedding, I am glad beyond words that Challenger has found someone who can breathe some life back into him.'

She laughed at the idea. 'If you think I am likely to bring about a change in his character, I fear you will be disappointed.' It was all she could do to maintain her own personality in his continued efforts to subdue her spirits.

'The fact that he married you is change enough for a start,' the Duke said. 'He has been far too proper since his return from Belgium.'

'You speak as if he was ever another way,' George said in disbelief.

The Duke gave her a surprised look. 'Very much so. I am surprised you did not know it already.'

'I know he is very conscious of scandal,' she said, trying not to reveal such profound ignorance of his character.

'Because of his family,' the Duke agreed. 'If you have not noticed it already, his parents and elder brother are horrible. When we were at Oxford, his method of dealing with them was quite the opposite of what it is now. His intention, as I remember it, was to outdo them all.'

'Frederick Challenger?' she said, doubting. 'Are you sure we speak of the same man?'

The Duke laughed again. 'How do you think he came to own such a notoriously decadent club? He courted scandal freely, in his youth.'

'Tell me more,' she said eagerly. 'I have seen nothing but propriety from him, since the day we met.'

The Duke nodded. 'You only know the Frederick Challenger that the army created. He is as disdainful of his family as he ever was, of course. But he thinks he must set a good example for his younger siblings and has got very good at giving and maintaining order.'

'I am well aware of that,' George said, with as little animosity as possible.

'Do not take him too seriously,' the Duke said, with a gentle smile. 'The rest of us do not.'

'I do not let myself be intimidated,' she said with a surprised smile. 'But I am un-accustomed to being encouraged in my mis-behaviour.'

He laughed, yet again, and stopped, as if surprised by the sound of it. 'You, my dear, are a breath of fresh air in this stale city. I have not been so amused in ages. It gives me reason to hope that you will blow the cobwebs off my friend as well. There is no reason for him to be as wild as he was. None of us are schoolboys any more. But that does not mean I wish him to be a joyless, hidebound old man.'

'He is not so bad…' She stopped herself, unable to defend him with a lie.

'He is still my friend,' Jacob assured her.

'But in recent years, I see no sign that he is enjoying his freedom. He is always at the club, yet he is always alone. We must hope that matrimony suits him better.'

If that was the goal, then they were all doomed. But the discussion raised interesting points. Perhaps she had not been the one who was wrong all this time. Perhaps he had his faults as well. 'I will do what I can for him,' she agreed. But the likelihood was that all she could be was a thorn in his side.

'Excellent. You must not change.'

Another dance was starting and he directed her to a set in need of a female before returning to the side of the room.

Fred had not thought that there could be such a thing as too much success. He'd maintained a careful watch over Georgiana for most of the evening, waiting for the inevitable disaster that would require a strategic retreat from the ball with a feigned megrim or family emergency.

But none had come. She laughed and chatted and danced nearly every dance, but stood up with no partner more than once. She was the epitome of grace and elegance. If appearance was everything, then he could not ask for a better wife. She was gliding across the room to him, now, offering an affectionate smile that he'd have sworn was sincere. Then she opened her mouth and spoiled it. 'Are you enjoying the evening, Mr Challenger?'

'Very much so.' The words sounded stiff and awkward, even to him.

She opened her fan with a snap and fluttered it in front of her face as if to hide her next words. 'Then I suggest you make some effort to prove it. People are beginning to remark on your behaviour.'

'My behav...?' She had turned away from him before he could even complete the word.

'Mrs Challenger?' A young buck he did not recognise was bowing low over his wife's hand.

'Lieutenant Williams,' she replied with a gracious smile.

'I have come to claim the dance you promised me this afternoon.'

'Of course.' Without another look in Fred's direction, she abandoned him and let the fellow lead her out on to the dance floor.

Who was he and how did she know him? More importantly, when had they been able to speak this afternoon? The young officer was one of many people who were strangers to him, but that his wife had greeted by name this evening. Some even addressed her as Georgiana. Fred was beginning to wonder if he was the only person in London who had not been acquainted with her, this Season.

He had no one to blame but himself. He'd had the chance and refused an introduction. In retrospect, that now seemed as foolish as telling her that he was not fond of dancing and had no intention of doing so tonight.

'At a ball to celebrate our wedding, you do not intend to dance.' Her eyes had flashed like a struck flint when he'd told her.

But he had not relented. The way he felt when he looked at her made it far too dangerous to be near her. Even standing beside her on the receiving line, the plans for simple separation seemed to erode like beach sand in a high tide. If they danced, they would end the evening in bed. And tomorrow, his life would no longer be his own. 'I will not dance,' he repeated.

The pride and confidence she'd displayed as he'd draped the chain about her neck all but disappeared. The sparks vanished. She was frightened, small, and about to shed a girl's tears of self-pity.

But only for a moment. She squared her shoulders, tossed her head, and smiled, looking directly into his eyes, ready to meet any challenge. 'Very well, then. But I do not expect to sit down, all evening. I will have to find other partners.'

He nodded approval and told her to dance as much as she wished. But it had never occurred to him how annoying it might be to see her take the hand of a handsome stranger closer to her age and wearing a uniform that had never seen battle.

'Your wife seems to be having a good time.' Jake had come to stand beside him to observe the dancing.

Fred grunted.

'I would have thought it would be you out there with her. Not tired of marriage after a mere few days, I hope.'

'You know I am not much of a dancer,' he said, draining his glass of wine and taking another from the tray of a passing servant.

'Save the lies for your wife. I have seen you dance happily and often.'

'Well, I do not feel like doing it tonight,'

he said, in a tone that should have ended the discussion.

'It has been less than three days since the wedding.' Jake said, thoughtfully. 'I suppose you have better things to do with your time.'

'I was at the club just last night,' Fred replied. 'I left early, of course. But once things are a bit more settled, I shall return to my responsibilities.'

Jake let loose with a bark of laughter. 'By all means, do not neglect the club. Heaven save me from idiots. If that is what has been occupying your mind in the first week of your marriage, then you do not deserve the lovely Georgiana.'

'You mean... You assumed that...' What must Jake think of the embarrassing flush that stole into his cheeks at the thought of bedding his wife? Fred was far too experienced to be acting like a bridegroom, but he could not seem to help himself.

'You are tired,' Jake said significantly, then glanced at the dancers. 'But she does not seem to be.'

'She is young,' Fred said, gritting his teeth. 'And I am not so young as I used to be.' That made her sound insatiable and him incapable.

But it was better than having the world think he had not touched her.

At this, Jake laughed all the harder. 'Then you should be spending more time in your bed. *Resting.*'

'Well...' Fred gave a helpless shrug.

'That is all right,' Jake assured him. 'I do not expect you to tell tales about married life. Georgiana is a wife, not a mistress. I promise, Oliver and I will treat her with the respect she deserves.' He glanced around the room and said glumly, 'Now that the dukedom has fallen to me, I suppose I shall be expected to find a bride of my own.' As usual, he did not sound in any way happy about his title or his future.

'It is not so bad to be married,' Fred replied, though he could not help sounding equally glum.

'Of course, if I had a mind to wed, I would want to pick someone just like Georgiana,' his friend said, pensively.

'Why?' Fred had not meant for the word to be so sudden and so utterly perplexed.

Jake gave him a surprised look. 'She is a lovely girl. One of the beauties of the Season. From what I have been told, it was a challenge to attract her attention.'

'A challenge.' Fred had not thought her such. As he had watched her making the rounds of balls and routs, she had seemed too free with her favours. She had been everywhere, danced with everyone, and was always surrounded by a throng of young men. Even though he'd tried to avoid her, she had always seemed to be underfoot, in his way, or staring daggers at him from across the room.

'There are a slew of men who have been trying to catch her for the better part of the Season,' Jake said. 'She showed not a bit of interest in anyone who offered. Of course, if it was because the two of you had been having secret trysts...' Jake left the sentence open as if waiting for a confidence to be revealed.

He was tempted to admit the truth. But it would not reflect well on the woman he had married that a good portion of London society had seen her barely dressed and bartering away her virtue. Better to hold his tongue. 'I am truly fortunate,' he agreed, feeling more confused than ever.

'She is exactly what you need.' Jake looked out at the dance floor, where Georgiana was laughing as she failed miserably at the steps of The Shipwreck'd Boy. It did not really matter how well she danced. Her partner looked thoroughly besotted to be near her. Didn't he know that she was recently married and supposedly devoted to someone else?

Fred frowned. Many times a neglected wife was seen as an opportunity. He knew from personal experience what flatteries to use that would turn the head of a woman with a mind to stray. How long would it be before his own wife found a favourite?

His stomach churned with a feeling that he'd have called jealousy, if he was the sort of person prone to such an emotion. More likely what he was feeling was a touch of wind from the pickled onions that had accompanied the buffet.

'I was better off as I was,' Fred muttered, before he could help himself. 'I had responsibility enough without adding a wife.'

'The weight of the world rested on your shoulders, I am sure,' Jake said in a cool tone to remind him that his current duties as a peer far outstripped any burden that Fred might complain about.

'I meant nothing by it,' Fred apologised quickly. 'It is just that things between Georgiana and myself are…more complicated than I imagined they would be.'

His friend smiled and nodded. 'That is exactly why you needed her. Lately, you take a simple thing like loving a beautiful woman and turn it into a difficulty. It is a good thing she does not seem so bothered by her marriage to you for, if I am honest, it is not all that pleasant to be around you. You act as though a single misstep will break that stiff neck of yours. I am the one in mourning, yet you smile even less than I do.'

Jake had few reasons to smile. Fred knew that he blamed himself for the accident that had killed both his father and brother, and landed him with an unexpected title. What did it say about Fred that he was a drag on the Duke's already low spirits? 'Do not waste time worrying about me,' he said, forcing a smile. 'You should be enjoying this evening as well. You spend even more time than you used to at Vitium et Virtus. And yet, if you mean to drink until dawn, the least you could do is join the crowd in the common rooms and not hide in the office with a bottle.'

If they had not been such old friends, the discussion might have ended in an argument.

Instead, there was a moment of silence that stood as a wordless apology. Then, Fred said, 'It is good that Oliver has still retained some of the buoyancy of youth. Where is he tonight?'

'Paris, I think. Trying to steal the entertainments from that French club he keeps talking about.'

'And while we are here behaving like gentlemen, he has a beautiful courtesan in one hand and a glass of France's finest brandy in the other,' Fred finished, unsure whether he felt envy, or relief that the job had fallen to someone else.

'I wonder, do you have the heart to continue as part of the management? Now that you are married…'

'I am as committed as I ever was,' Fred said firmly. 'We agreed that we would keep the place running, so that it might be here when Nick returns.'

'Or to honour his memory,' Jake added, expressing the doubt that they both secretly shared.

'The club was his idea. He had the greatest stake in the place,' Fred reminded him. 'If he is alive, we must see to it that his investment is thriving, when he returns.'

'And I will burn in hell before I allow Bowles to take over that empty chair,' Jake said, frowning. 'He was bothering me about it again last month.'

Fred shook his head. 'The fellow is a loathsome little toady and I like him no better now than I did at Oxford. But just as important as his lack of character is the fact that he has not a feather to fly with. He was forced to run for the country, one step ahead of his debt collectors.'

Jake smiled. 'It is no less than he deserved.'

'Should Bowles return, I have no intention of leaving a second empty chair at Vitium et Virtus for him to aspire to. I assure you, my recent marriage will have no effect on my activities,' Fred said, feeling more trapped than ever by both the club and the woman.

'Of course it won't, my love.' His wife was standing before him, hands on hips. Fred hoped he was the only one who could hear the irony in her voice as she announced her affection for him. 'No matter my opinions on the subject, I expect you will be just as firmly attached to Vitium et Virtus as you are now.'

'If you have opinions on the club, you should refrain from mentioning them in public,' he said automatically. 'You should not even know that the place exists.'

'Then I will pretend that I have not heard people whispering about it, everywhere I go,' she said, shaking her head in disbelief as if he were the one who was naïve.

Then she leaned towards Jake and said in a conspiratorial whisper, 'Is it true that husbands and wives arrive there together and go off with others as easily as changing partners in a dance?'

'I would not know,' Jake said with a wink. 'I am not married.'

'I do not think I should like to find out from experience,' she replied.

The remark surprised him. Did it arise from actual loyalty, or was she merely feigning devotion?

Then she finished, 'One husband is more than enough for me.'

Before Fred could respond, she smiled at the Duke and asked, 'Are you also preoccupied with that club, even tonight, Your Grace? The room is full of young ladies, eager to stand up with you.'

In response, Jake turned pink about the ears and his answer had a slight hesitation that almost sounded like nerves. 'I thought we agreed to be on familiar terms. You need not bother with the formality of a title if we are to be friends.'

'Jacob, then,' she said, smiling even more brightly.

When had they agreed on familiarity? As far as Fred knew, they had not known each other at all before the wedding. Despite his desire to see his friend be happy, it made him uneasy to see the easy smiles that passed between them after so limited an acquaintance.

'Do you mean to hold up the wall with my husband, Jacob? Or do you plan to dance?'

'We are not the only men in the room,' Fred said, trying to catch her eye and remind her of the black mourning gloves his friend was wearing, even at his own ball. 'Surely they can find someone else.'

'I believe I have danced with nearly every other man in the room,' she said. 'Now, it is only manners that I should dance with our host.' She gave Fred an appraising look and held out a hand to him. 'Unless you have changed your mind and wish to reclaim me.'

He stared at it for a moment, but made no move. For all the bravery he had shown in battle, why did he hesitate now?

It did not matter. He had waited too long to give his answer and she'd turned back to his friend, holding out her hands. 'Your Gr… I mean, Jacob, will you dance with me?'

His friend hesitated for a moment, then smiled back. 'I had not planned to stand up. But a single dance with an honoured guest is not so very shocking. And I know better than to refuse such an opportunity.'

Was this a dig at him? It was too late to tell. The pair was already gone, arm in arm, to take their place in the set for the next dance.

They made a handsome couple and it was clear that dancing did Jake good. His step was light and he chatted easily with Georgiana as they moved down the row of couples. It was just the sort of thing Fred would have hoped for the fellow a week or two ago. Why did it annoy him now? And why was he feeling the same tightening in his guts that could no longer be attributed to indigestion?

Could it really be jealousy? He had known Jake since they were seven. Even at such times as they'd both fancied the same girl, there was never a question that a romantic attachment would supersede their friendship. One would happily step out of the way if the other had a deeper feeling.

But neither of them had been married before. Suppose Jake took a liking to Georgiana? And suppose she favoured him as well? As her stepmother had been so eager to point out, his wife had hated him before they married. He had given her little reason to change her opinion of him since.

Without intending to, he took a step forward, half ready to go out on to the floor, grab her by the hand, and lead her back to his side. How foolish would that have been? He'd be making just the sort of scene he hated from the rest of his family. He drank deeply, wishing the champagne was something strong enough to chase the madness out of his head.

And then, they were back, winded and happy, taking their places on either side of him as if nothing had happened. 'Your friend is a delightful dancer,' she said with a smile.

'As is your wife,' Jake added, looking truly envious.

'Not that Frederick would know about such a thing.' Georgiana gave him another challenging look.

'Not know?' Jake was looking at him in surprise. 'I was under the impression that the two of you had been carrying on a secret romance for some time now. You must have danced together at least once.'

'It has been quite some while,' Fred said, wishing they had taken the time to create a believable past between them.

'And Frederick is far too serious to dance.' Georgiana was pouting at him.

'He did not used to be so,' Jake supplied. 'I remember a time when he was the first to take the floor and the last to leave it.'

'I bet he does not even know how to waltz,' Georgiana taunted, fluttering her fan. 'I do. I was not supposed to, of course. But I would not let prudery stop me from something so pleasant.'

'Young ladies should not dance so close with men,' Fred said automatically. 'It is not proper.'

'But I am an old, married lady,' she reminded him. 'No one will look twice if I do it now.'

I would.

'And I have waltzed,' he added. 'At the Duchess of Richmond's ball, before Waterloo.' When they had got word of Napoleon's approach, he had jumped into the saddle still wearing his dancing slippers.

The pair of them were staring at him, expectantly.

At last, Jake said, 'Well?'

The band was striking up a waltz. It would look strange for a supposedly happy couple not to be dancing something that gave them a chance to hold each other in public. Perhaps someone had noticed already. By avoiding her, he was still managing to cause gossip. He wet his lips, suddenly nervous. 'May I have this dance, my dear?'

Now, she was the one hesitating, making him wonder if she meant to refuse. Then she smiled as mischievously as she had at Jake and curtsied. 'Of course, my love.'

He offered his hand and led her out on to the floor, pulling her easily into his arms.

Other than the brief kiss on their wedding night, he had not held her so closely since that night in the club. At the thought, his blood rushed and he felt the beginnings of an autonomic reaction totally inappropriate for a grown man in a public place. He schooled his thoughts, counting out the multiplication tables in his head until he could regain control.

'Do not feel it necessary to make polite conversation with me while we dance. Now that we are married, such banal courtesies are not required.' She was smiling, but her words stung like thorns in his flesh.

'Do you normally speak without regard for your partner's feelings as you dance?' he asked, leaning closer to whisper softly into her ear as he had at breakfast.

'Is your sensibility so delicate that you cannot withstand a single comment?'

Strangely, he felt more at ease the longer they argued. 'I prefer to think of myself as discerning,' he replied, twirling her. 'I would not normally dance with a woman who only wished to insult me.'

'I suspect you would cut her dead before she got the chance to even meet you,' she replied.

'And she would never let me forget it, even if I regretted it after.' Even as he spoke them, the words came as a surprise. How different might their lives have been had he accepted her introduction and danced with her months ago?

'Is this an apology?' she said, shocked out of her sarcasm.

'Now that I have met your stepmother, I think it might have been unfair to blame you for the rudeness on our first meeting, or some of the disturbances I witnessed since.'

'Thank you,' she whispered.

The hand he was holding gave his an affectionate squeeze.

'And now that you have tested it, does my dancing meet with your approval?' He gave her another quick spin in his arms and gathered her close again.

She responded with a gasp of delight. 'You are a very good dancer. Perhaps the best partner I've ever had.'

'It is good to know I can get you to follow, in this at least.' He said it gently, so she might know he was only teasing. 'And thank you for your opinion of my abilities. From now on, when you are dancing with another, remember this moment and come back to me.'

He'd always had confidence in his powers of seduction. But tonight, he was almost afraid that she would dismiss him as unmemorable. He held his breath, awaiting her response.

She gave him a dazed nod. Instead of her usual look of suspicion or disgust, she was staring at him as if he was the hero some claimed he had been. The music was ending, but the moment was too precious to relinquish. 'Shall we take a walk on the terrace?' he said, glancing towards the open French doors.

'The room is stifling,' she agreed, though as she said it, she shivered. In anticipation, perhaps?

'Let us go, then.' He had thought to say 'come with me', but those words sounded too much like a command. If they ended up in the same place, was it really any different if they went side by side rather than one following the other?

She linked her arm in his as if she could not be prouder to have him for an escort and they escaped the room together.

On the other side of the doors, it was a different world. The candlelight gave way to darkness, the music to the sound of nightjars and crickets. The stale smell of too many bodies jammed together in a small space was replaced with the fragrance from pots of night-blooming jasmine decorating the low railing that gave way to the garden.

Georgiana drew closer to him, shivering again, as if asking him to share the warmth of his body. The proper thing to do would be to return to the ballroom for a wrap. But was it really necessary to be proper at all times? The moon was full, the night romantic, and there was a beautiful girl in his arms waiting to be kissed.

He leaned forward, ready to oblige.

She touched a finger to his lips, holding him back. 'We mustn't.'

'Why?' He touched the finger with his tongue.

'It is not polite. We are guests of the Duke.'

Nothing personal, then. Just his own rules, coming back to haunt him. 'He will not mind if he does not know.' Fred leaned forward again.

'But if someone sees us. Think of the scandal.'

'Scandal be damned,' he said, lunging forward and pressing her close.

She gave one brief squeak of alarm before succumbing to the kiss, meeting his tongue eagerly with her own. 'Mr Challenger,' she murmured when he allowed her time to breathe.

'Mrs Challenger?' he answered, mocking her formality and cupping one of her breasts with his hand.

By the way she stiffened in surprise, he could tell she had not been touched that way before. 'No,' she whispered, but she was laughing as she said it, as if it was not a denial at all.

'No?' he asked, releasing her and instead

rubbing his knuckles back and forth across the sensitive nipple he could feel pebbling beneath the fabric of her bodice.

'Well…' She trapped his hand with her own, pressing it more tightly to her.

'That's what I thought you meant,' he said and pulled her deeper into the shadows of the house. When he was sure they were hidden by the darkness, he dipped his mouth to her neckline, following the edge of the fabric to search for the flesh his hand had excited.

'No,' she whispered again, still laughing. But her fingers were tickling the hair at the back of his neck, stroking his nape to reward him for his daring.

'Just one kiss,' he whispered back, waiting until he felt the gentle pressure of her hand urging him on. He lowered his head further, his tongue searching for her nipple. When he found it, he felt the flutter of her heart against his cheek and the flutter of her fingers in his hair. Then she pulled one hand away, covering her own mouth to stifle a gasp as he kissed her breast, languid and tantalising, but as he had promised, only once. She took a shuddering breath, like a woman on the edge of climax.

Though he knew he must, he did not want

to release her. Until they were home and alone, one kiss was all either of them could withstand. Be damned to his foolish promise of marital celibacy. He would have his wife this very night. He would give her what they both wanted. Once desire was sated, they could discuss the future with minds unclouded by lust.

With a sigh of his own, he raised his head and pulled the neckline of her gown up again. Then he leaned her back in his arms to kiss her lips. When he released her, she sagged against the nearest wall as if ready to swoon. So he caught her again, holding her close and resting his cheek against hers.

From behind them, he heard a low chuckle and a cleared throat.

They broke instantly. He stuffed his hands into his pockets to resist touching her again. She made a hurried examination of her garments, hands travelling down her bodice to be sure that everything was in place.

'I wondered where you two had got to,' Jake drawled, staring deliberately out into the garden.

Fred felt a moment's embarrassment before remembering that Jake had caught him doing things far more scandalous than kissing a girl in the moonlight. But it had been years since he had behaved so.

And the woman in question had never mattered before. Georgiana was his wife. It was his job to protect her from scandal, not to lead her into it. He did not want his friends thinking of her as the sort of woman who would entertain the advances of a man like the one he used to be.

Georgiana had turned to examine her reflection carefully in the window, as if searching for any trace of what they had done together. She would find none, he was sure, other than a slight flush on her cheeks. All the same, she muttered something about the need to go to the retiring room and hurried past the Duke, back into the ballroom.

'I told you she would do you good,' Jake said, smiling after her.

Fred stared after her, still wondering if that was true.

Perhaps her husband liked her after all.

For the rest of the evening, George did her best to regain her composure, chatting amiably with the gentlemen who danced with her and sharing gossip with the ladies they escorted. But what she actually wanted to do was to follow Frederick Challenger around the room like a moonstruck girl.

Her head was in the clouds after the waltz. Her body tingled from the kiss on the terrace. The little part of her mind that was capable of coherent thought was focused on what was likely to come, once they got home. After discovery by the Duke, they needed to be discreet for the rest of the evening. That was probably why Frederick was distant but polite to her once he returned to the ballroom.

But once they were home and could be alone, everything would change. He had admitted he was wrong about her, while they'd danced. If he could change his opinion, then so could she. He was still rather stuffy, of course. And too concerned with the opinions of others.

But Jacob had said that Frederick had not always been that way. When he forgot himself, as he had on the terrace, she liked him better. A single goodnight kiss might be all that was necessary to renew his life and change hers. Now that they were finally on the way home, he lounged in the carriage seat opposite hers, his face in shadows.

'I had a nice evening,' she said, smiling to let him know that he was part of the reason for her happiness.

'That is good,' he said, but made no effort to give his opinion of the ball.

She touched the necklace he had given her, running her fingers down the chain to her bosom. 'And I like your gift. It is very pretty.'

'You are very pretty.' The compliment surprised her, for she'd already begun to fear that he was going to pretend nothing had happened between them.

'Thank you.' She spread her fingers across her bodice. 'Do you like my new gown? It is more daring than I am used to.'

His answer to this was nothing more than low, hoarse breathing. But it was proof that Polly had been right. It was easier than she'd thought to influence a man, even one as proper as Mr Challenger.

She toyed with the necklace again. 'I had planned to make Polly take it up. But Caroline insisted that it was no different than all the other women were wearing…'

'Caroline?' He scrambled to sit upright as if trying to put more distance between them.

'Viscountess Linholm,' she said, though it

should not have been necessary to remind him of his own sister-in-law.

'What were you doing with my brother's wife?' For a moment, a ray of moonlight struck his face. In the pale, white glow he looked almost angry.

'Shopping,' she said. 'I believe it was what you demanded of me, just this morning.'

'I never gave you permission to associate with *that woman*,' he said, as if the very sound of her name might be poisonous.

'*That woman* is a member of your family,' she said. 'And my family as well, now that we are married.'

'I forbid you to see her again,' he said. She did not need daylight to know that his expression was as stern as it ever had been.

'Forbid me? If you were a normal man, you'd be encouraging me to visit her.' More than that, she had thought it would make him happy. Why had she bothered to try?

Now he was leaning towards her, not in love, but in menace. 'Stay away from Caroline and my brother as well.'

'Which brother?' she said, trying to hide her hurt in sarcasm. 'You have two of them, I believe.'

'Caroline's husband,' he said briefly, as if she were being deliberately obtuse.

'And what of your sisters? I saw them as well, today. Are they a corrupting influence on me? Or do you fear I shall ruin them?'

'Judge for yourself,' he retorted. 'I doubt my sisters were responsible for the horde of men that were swarming after you all night.'

'They were not a horde,' she said. But there had been a great many introductions made at Steven's. Even though he had no reason to fear, she had been sure her husband would be angry.

But he was not just angry. He was furious beyond all sense. 'Can I not let you out of the house, even for an afternoon, without you coming home with an immodest gown, trailing half a regiment of admirers?'

'If you had a problem with my dress, you had but to say so and I'd have changed before we left the house.' Instead, he had draped her in gold and kissed her.

But he was far past seeing reason, near to shouting in rage. 'I warned you not to flaunt your indiscretions in front of me. And now, in the first week...'

'Indiscretions?' She could not help a surprised laugh. 'I danced at a ball with men that had been introduced to me by a member of your family. If I was indiscreet with anyone, it was with you.'

'Do not worry, madam. It will not happen again.' He rapped his cane on the side of the coach and called out to the driver. 'Wilson. Stop, immediately.'

They were passing Jermyn Street. If she looked out of the window, she could almost see the black lacquered door of Vitium et Virtus. 'Don't you dare,' she said, regretting it immediately. She had nothing to threaten him with other than to announce that it would make her cry. And by the tight feeling at the back of her throat, she was likely to do so no matter what he did.

'Since you have no care for propriety, why should I?' he said. Then he opened the door and leapt to the street without the help of a groom, slamming it behind him. As if he had not embarrassed her enough, he shouted to the coachman in a voice loud enough for half the street to hear. 'Take Mrs Challenger home, Wilson. And see that she stays there.'

Chapter Twelve

The next morning, George came downstairs to find the breakfast table set for one. It was not a surprise as much as a confirmation of what she already knew. She had been awake most of the night, alternately crying into her pillow and listening for a step on the stair that had had never come.

When it came time to rise, Polly fussed over her red-rimmed eyes offering cool cloths, powdering her nose and allowing her to pretend that it was the beginning of a cold and not the end of an argument with a man she had never meant to care about. If Mr Challenger worried so much about the opinions of the servants, he should not have behaved in a way that informed the household, from stable groom to scullery maid, that he hated his wife and refused to stay in the same house with her.

His prolonged absence and the lack of explanation for it was precisely the sort of marriage she'd expected to have. If he had given her the life she had asked for on their wedding day, she would not have shed a single tear over him. She might have retreated from London entirely. In the country, with no *ton* to gossip about her, there would be no need to worry about social missteps and ruined reputations. Nor would she have to care about what her husband did when he was not at home. He could have spent every night of his life at Vitium et Virtus and she would have neither known nor cared.

Instead, he had tried to seduce her. At least, she assumed that was what had been happening. His behaviour had been very confusing. When she had come down the stairs, he'd acted as if he liked her, smiling and giving her gifts. Then, they'd arrived at the ball and he'd been purposely difficult, refusing to have fun. Then he'd changed his mind and agreed to dance.

The waltz had been magical. He had murmured apologies while holding her in his arms and gazing into her eyes. She had never wanted it to end. Then, they'd gone to the terrace.

Her heart beat quicker at the memory. She could still feel his kiss on her breast. It had been scandalous, but he had been the one to suggest it. Nay, he had insisted. He had been reckless as she tried to be the responsible one. It was not a role she was good at and she had never been so happy to fail.

Once they got home, she had been sure that there would at least be more kissing. Quite possibly, there would be other, even better things, but she had no idea what they would be. He had admitted that he had been wrong about her and was showing signs of becoming less strict. It was as if she had suddenly discovered she had married a handsome, loving gentleman and not Frederick Challenger at all.

But when they'd set out for home, he been worse than his usual, disapproving self. He had been irrationally angry and accused her of things that made no sense at all. Had the kisses on the terrace been some sort of test? If so, she had failed it. Or did the Challenger family have some streak of madness that he had stopped trying to fight against? Or perhaps, whatever was about to change between them was as great a mystery to him as it was to her.

The breakfast room door opened and the butler stopped just inside the threshold. 'A visitor, ma'am. Mr Challenger.'

'Bring him to me immediately.' None of that mattered any more. She turned towards the door with a smile, ready to forgive him, without another thought. Then, she remembered that Jenks would never have introduced his own master as a guest.

Christian Challenger stepped into the room, clearly as surprised to see her as she was him. 'I expected Fred,' he said by way of introduction.

'Hello, Mr Challenger,' she said as a gentle reminder of a proper greeting.

'Mrs Challenger,' he said, stumbling over the words.

'Please, call me George,' she said, allowing her brother-in-law a familiarity that she had not yet heard from her husband. 'Frederick is not here this morning. Would you like to join me for breakfast?'

He hesitated.

Before he could find a way to escape, she signalled a footman to set him a place.

At last, Christian surrendered, thanked her for her hospitality, filled his plate, and ate his eggs in silence.

When he offered no explanation for his visit, she asked, 'Was there something that you wished to speak to your brother about? And can I help in any way?'

'I came to apologise,' he said, looking glumly into his coffee.

'Whatever for?'

'I was imprudent,' Christian said, still not looking up.

'Everyone is, from time to time,' George agreed, wondering if her husband set the same rules for his younger siblings as he did for his wife.

Christian nodded. 'But our family has a reputation for it. Frederick has always said if I wish people to think better of me, I must take care to moderate my behaviour.'

'That is nothing more than common sense,' George said. 'I fail to see what good it does for Frederick to lecture you on a thing which you will discover for yourself.'

Christian looked at her as if this had not occurred to him.

'You are of age, are you not?' she prompted.

He nodded.

'And you do fewer foolish things than you used to, I expect.'

'Of course,' he agreed.

'Then the trend will likely continue. You

will grow into just the sort of responsible and respected gentleman you have always wished to be. But until then you must allow yourself the occasional mistake without worrying that others will think ill of you.'

'Frederick has never made mistakes,' Christian said with bitterness.

'I am sure he has,' George said. If his absence today was an indication, he still considered their marriage to be one of them. 'He pretends he has not. But he is mortal, therefore he is as fallible as the rest of us.' When her brother-in-law still looked doubtful, she added, 'I am his wife and know him better than you.'

The last was an enormous lie, but Christian seemed to relax a little upon hearing it. Then he frowned. 'That is all well and good. But I doubt reminding him of his own fallibility will encourage him to help me out of the mess I've made.'

'Tell me about it,' she said. 'Perhaps there is something I can do.'

'I have run through my entire month's allowance at the tables of that damned club of his,' Christian said in frustration. 'When he hears of it, I am sure to get a lecture about my irresponsibility. It will be all the worse when I have to borrow my rent money from him later.'

Having received a week's worth of Mr Challenger's moralising, she could not help but feel sympathy for him. 'Is there no way to win the money back without telling him?' she asked.

'They will not take a marker at Vitium et Virtus,' he said. 'Since I have no cash, they will bar me from the room.'

A thought occurred to her. 'I have money,' she said. Quite a bit of it, really, even after what she had spent at the dressmaker's.

'I could not take your household money,' he said. 'Suppose I lost it?'

'Then I will say that it was all my fault,' George said. Considering his current opinion of her, Mr Challenger would have no trouble believing it.

But, suppose she did something so terrible that he wanted to pack her off to the country? He'd said they must remain in town until people had no reason to comment on their sudden marriage. But if he refused to spend his nights at home, gossip was inevitable and not her fault at all. Yesterday morning, he had hinted that he would sleep in the same bed with her as if it was a punishment. But it was clearly an empty threat.

And one day later, an opportunity was presenting itself that would both help the young Mr Challenger regain his allowance, while making his elder brother so incandescent with rage. No matter what he did to her after, it had to be better than the humiliation of last night's sudden departure.

She looked at her husband's brother and smiled. 'Do not worry, Christian. I have a plan that will render your indiscretion insignificant by comparison.'

Fred settled back in his chair in the owners' suite and raised a toast to Nick's empty place before drinking. He had lost count of the number of brandies he'd had since arriving at the club in the wee hours of the morning. But several of those drinks had been necessary to convince himself that the room he had chosen upstairs was as comfortable as his own home. A mattress designed for fornication did not always provide a good night's sleep. And the lurid pictures on the wall provided a constant reminder of the things he was not doing with the woman who had been near to fainting in his arms scant hours before.

If she had been anyone else's wife but his own, the way forward with Georgiana would have been a simple one. Bed her and forget her. But marriage was complicated. Despite what Georgiana had been hoping for, one could not totally forget one's own spouse when it became convenient to do so. After even a single night of bliss, there might be a child to contend with. And his parents, who could hardly stand the sight of each other, were frequently forced into each other's company at social gatherings.

After losing his head on the terrace, Fred had stopped to consider what consummating his marriage might mean. But each time he had tried to list the problems it might create, he had glanced at Georgiana—an eager, responsive and carnally curious beauty—and he had been ready to risk his future for a few minutes of passion. He'd sat in the carriage, at war with his own common sense, watching as she touched the breast he had kissed as if coaxing him to do it again.

He had wanted to refuse her and retreat back into the safe distance they'd maintained from each other since their first meeting, but it was too late for that. He was lost. When they arrived home, they would make love. He would worry about tomorrow when it came.

Then she had invoked the name of the demon from his past and he'd realised what he should have known long ago. It was happening again, just as it had before.

A beautiful woman on the dance floor, beckoning to him to come closer. Closer still. A few moments in her arms and his life had changed for ever.

The last time he had been at Vitium et Virtus and not some society gathering. The woman in his arms had been masked. In the heady atmosphere of the room, what had started as a waltz became not so much a dance as a seduction set to music. He had taken her lips as she had shamelessly rubbed her body against his, not caring who saw. The bodice of her gown had been so low that her nipples were clearly visible, erect from teasing against the hair of his chest as they moved.

He had kissed her neck. Her hand had moved lower, caressing him through the fabric of his trousers and leaving no doubt what she wanted from him. It had been no different from a hundred other nights at the club and they were no different from a half-dozen couples on the floor with them that very night.

He'd whispered a suggestion that they go upstairs.

She had taken him by the hand, not just willing, but eager, tumbling with him through the first open door of rooms kept for casual joinings. She'd shed her gown before he'd even managed to close the door and was tugging at his shirt to pull it over his head, stroking his back and trailing hot kisses up and down the bare flesh.

'Frederick, I want you.'

She had known him, despite his mask. But was that really so surprising? He was there almost every night. Many of the members knew him from life outside the club. His identity had to be an open secret.

'And who are you, my darling?' He'd reached for her mask as well, the only scrap of fabric left between her and complete nudity. Who was she? He had to know. A woman of such passion, such enthusiasm, such a prodigious appetite, was not someone he wanted to forget after one night.

She had turned away from his grasp to kiss her way down his belly, undoing the flap of his breeches with steady and experienced hands. She kissed like a courtesan, familiar with the needs of a man, and happy to fulfil them.

She tormented him with her hands and tongue until finally, he'd picked her up bodily and tossed her on to the bed, if only to have a chance to finish undressing.

When he'd turned back, the mask had slipped, giving him his first glimpse of her face.

His brother's wife lay before him, legs spread, her own hand tangling in the chestnut curls between them. 'Frederick,' she'd said breathlessly and held the other hand out to him in welcome.

He had grabbed his breeches and run. And he had not stopped running until Waterloo.

He filled his glass and spoke to the place Nick should have occupied, wishing that his spirit might be there to hear his confession. 'If you can hear me, old friend, come back to us and take the burden of this place from me. I have lost the stomach to take pleasure in it. And now...'

He shook his head, amazed that he could be so easily tricked. In a single afternoon, Caroline had transformed the sweet, awkward girl he'd married into the sophisticated temptress that had all the men in the room dancing attendance on her, including him.

When he'd called her out for her behaviour, she'd had the gall to argue, quite logically, that there was no way she could have known a family visit would displease him. She'd said that he was being the irrational one.

Then, he'd proved her point by running away, just as he had after the incident with Caroline. There had been no reason for it. She was his own wife, not someone else's. The disagreement between them could not be settled if he did not go home to talk to her. He would have to, eventually. But what would he say to her when he did?

'Mr Challenger, there is a problem in the game room.' Snyder, the porter, stood in the doorway, arms folded across his chest, but head dipped in deference, as if sorry for the intimidating figure he could not help but present.

'Handle it,' Fred said, tired to the bone of difficulties created by other people's lack of control.

'It is Mr Christian,' Snyder said, waiting to see if the instructions had changed now that Fred knew it was his brother causing the problem. 'He has been playing all evening and is losing rather badly.'

'And where did he get the money to do that?' Frederic said, giving the porter a dark look. 'Westmoor said he left here the other night with nothing but lint in his pockets.' He had been expecting a contrite visit from the boy on that very subject. Nothing would prevent future excesses faster than having to beg for a loan to cover them.

Then, a terrible thought occurred to him. 'No one here gave him credit, did they?'

'No, Mr Challenger,' Snyder said, frowning. 'There is a lady with him.'

A woman, perhaps. But whether she was a lady was yet to be determined. In his mind, Fred sorted through a list of opera dancers and courtesans that Christian had associated with. All were either too poor or too sensible to give money back to the man who was supposed to be keeping them. That meant the woman staking him was likely older, perhaps a widow, but more likely the wife of a gentleman.

Christian was nearly three-and-twenty, old enough to make his own way in the world. But Fred could not simply stand by and watch the fellow ruin himself on some Jezebel at Vitium et Virtus. He had learned for himself the dangers of alluring women in masks and the way a single night with the wrong one could alter one's life for ever.

It was also his job to prevent scandals that would reflect poorly upon the club. If something Christian did here led to a duel with a jealous husband or, God forbid, caused him to blow his brains out over bad debts and a heartless jade, it would be Fred's fault for not stopping him sooner.

'Very well. I will take care of him, you deal with the woman.' He pulled himself out of the chair and walked to the gaming room with Snyder following a step behind.

When they arrived, it was just as the porter had said. Christian was at the tables with but a single chip left in front of him. He also lacked the common sense to be upset by the fact that he had squandered everything he had. He turned to the woman next to him, a blonde in low-cut, scarlet satin. 'I am out of money, again.'

'Help yourself,' she said, pushing half of her large pile of chips in his direction. Then she shuffled the cards in her hand with the facility of a dockside gambler and began to deal.

'It is not right that the two of you should collude,' grumbled another player. 'We are playing drumhead, not whist.'

'We are not colluding,' the woman replied with a smile and tossed a handful of chips in his direction as well. 'I am beating him. I shall win those back from him and you as well, just as I did the last time.'

'The hell you will.' Fred stared at his brother's companion and thought longingly of that time, just a few days ago, when her voice had not been as familiar to him as his own.

Georgiana looked up at him, tipping her chin up defiantly, and half closing the blue eyes in her disguised face. 'I fail to see why not. The gentlemen at this table tonight lack both luck and skill.'

'Put down the cards and leave immediately, or by God...' Words failed him. He turned to his brother. 'And you!'

Christian shrugged. 'There is no harm in letting her play another hand. She has not lost once since arriving at the table. She has the devil's own luck.' And now, he was looking at her with the same awed smile that Fred had seen on his friends when they'd spoken of her.

'She has something of the devil, at least,' Fred agreed.

'And her husband is a very lucky man,' Christian said, with admiration.

Was it some sort of divine punishment that his brother was looking at his wife in a way that was practically lustful? When it had happened to Fred, it had been an accident. But Christian *knew*.

And so did Georgiana. She was the one at fault, here. Now she was smiling at him as if it pleased her to see him angry. 'Are you trying to decide how many of your rules have been broken?' She reached into her reticule and removed a small notebook and pencil. 'I think the answer is likely all of them. But it might help if you keep score on paper.'

'Perhaps you should be the one keeping a tally. I know for a fact your husband forbade you from setting foot in this place.'

She shrugged. 'I do not like it when he comes here, either. But what can be done about that?'

'This is not the place to discuss it,' he whispered. A few more words and everyone here would guess her identity and assume he had been cuckolded before the wedding cake had gone stale.

'Where and when?' she said, staring up at him without blinking. 'I see no reason to go home just to talk to the walls of an empty house.'

'But that is where you are going, all the same,' he said, in the quiet voice he used when dealing with drunkards and hysterical courtesans. 'Snyder, put this woman in a cab.'

Christian rose, ready to protect her. 'She came with me.'

'And she is leaving alone,' Fred said, putting a hand on the insolent puppy's shoulder and pushing him firmly back into his chair. 'I want to know that she arrives safely where she has been sent.'

It had been a coarse and stupid thing to say, for it implied he trusted neither wife nor brother. Christian was giving him a militant glare, ready to add insult to insult. Without intending to, Fred had created just the situation he'd feared.

A feminine laugh cut the tension between them. 'Christian, darling, remember what we spoke of? Now be a dear and collect my winnings. I will see you soon.' Then she turned to Snyder and accepted his arm, allowing him to escort her from the room.

Chapter Thirteen

It had been less than a week since the wedding and it was time to admit Fred's plan for a scandal-free marriage was a total failure.

He might not have minded her visit to Vitium et Virtus if his wife had had the decency to lose her allowance like the flighty chit she pretended to be. Then, she might have returned home shamefaced and sorrowful, ready to come to heel and behave like a lady.

Instead, she returned with a reticule that contained all of her money and all of Christian's as well. He'd have shouted at his brother for being a cloth-headed fool, if it had not been Fred's own wife who had fleeced the boy. Instead, he'd behaved like a jealous lover and very nearly provoked a duel.

Since it was his fault that Georgiana had joined their family, he was responsible for the damage she caused. Instead of scolding him about the dangers of gambling, Fred had apologised for his temper and written Christian a cheque for the money he'd lost, promising to say no more about it.

By the time he had mended the quarrel and come home, Georgiana was asleep in her own bed and the door to the room was locked as it always was.

A visit to his parents' home this morning had proved she was a bad influence on his sisters as well. Georgiana had encouraged them to buy Minerva novels and admitted that she was in the habit of hiding them in the cover of her prayer book so she might read them during chapel. Apparently, it was too late to forbid her to go to a prize fight. She had found her way into one before their marriage and described the action to Josephine in graphic detail.

Worst of all, she'd bought them a mynah bird that might have been the devil's own servant judging by the words it knew. Though his sisters assumed it spoke nonsense, he'd been in Portugal long enough to know what a shout of '*Ola, puta!*' meant. When the bird had greeted his mother with the phrase, he had snorted his tea through his nose.

He'd been leg-shackled to a disaster. But everywhere he went, from White's to Vitium et Virtus, people were congratulating him. They patted him on the back, shook her hand, and bought drinks so they might toast to his good fortune at marrying such a thoroughly delightful girl.

Fred had no choice but to thank them and agree. But all the while, he feared that his smile, which should be the smug grin of a recently bedded groom, was actually the nervous rictus of a man trapped in a minefield.

And with each moment he spent with her, the chance increased that he might drag her to the floor and ravish her on the spot. Last night, as he'd raged at her before throwing her from the club, he'd caught himself looking down her bodice and wondering what it would be like to carry her, still masked, to an upstairs bedroom and take her against a bedpost. When he'd got home, he'd spent half the night listening through the wall to her even breathing and wondering what she'd worn to bed.

And this morning, before his call on his mother, he'd glanced in a shop window and seen something that would suit her so well he'd purchased it immediately. What sort of fool bought apology presents before the argument had even begun?

He had to get her out of the city. London might have space for well over a million people, but it could not hold both Georgiana and his sanity. He would ensconce her in his country house in Richmond and escape as soon as she was settled, giving her the separate arrangements she had wanted from the first.

There would be no discussion of the matter, or lectures for her to ignore, no more ultimatums or threats of punishment. He would give her no chance to disobey. When she came down to breakfast, he would tell her of his plans and order her back upstairs to pack her clothes. There would be pouting and foot-dragging, and more than a few childish tears. It would be just as it was with his mother and sisters, if they were denied even a day of the London Season. Half the gentlemen at the club this month were hiding from wives and daughters who had forced them to remain in the city until the last ball had ended.

But he was not some weak-willed, weak-kneed fellow who could be swayed on the subject. If she was not ready in an hour, he would throw her over his shoulder and make her leave here with nothing but the clothes on her back.

He heard her approach on the stairs, light, almost skipping as she came down to the breakfast room. She was whistling.

He winced. Weren't women supposed to sing? All his sisters had been trained to do so. If Georgiana was capable of a solo, he had not heard it. Nor had he seen her drawing, or practising an instrument. But she was doing a creditable whistled version of a Mozart minuet, hopping down the last few steps in time to the end of a line. Her arrival on the landing seemed to jar her out of tune, which resulted in a laugh, and a series of bird whistles that ended in a slow, falling note as she arrived in the doorway to see him there.

'Good morning,' he said and glared at her.

After a moment of genuine surprise at his presence, she returned an equally dark, mocking frown. 'And good morning to you, Major Challenger. What a surprise to find you here.'

'It is my home,' he reminded her.

'And yet you chose to stay at Vitium et Virtus these last two nights,' she replied as if she had reason to be incensed by it.

'I belong there,' he said. 'You do not. In light

of your scandalous visit last night, I have decided that we will leave for my house in Richmond this morning.'

Her frown disappeared instantly. But rather than turn to the confusion or irritation he'd been prepared for, it became the breathtaking smile that had dazzled half of London. 'At last.' She darted past him to grab a piece of toast from the rack on the table, slathering it with marmalade and taking a bite. 'I will write a note to Father to tell him of my departure and will set Polly to packing immediately. If she cannot be done by the time the carriage is to set off, I will box her ears and leave directions for her to follow tomorrow.' She turned and was halfway out the door before he could stop her.

'Georgiana!'

She turned back to stare at him, tapping her foot as if impatient to be about her business.

'You have no complaints to this?' he asked, trying not to sound as confused as he felt.

She gave him an arch look, then shook her head, still chewing her breakfast. 'None.'

'I am not interfering with your schedule? You have no plans?'

'Nothing I cannot send regrets for,' she said, the picture of reason.

'You would not prefer London?'

'I have *seen* London,' she said. 'Every last inch of every house. But I have never seen your country home.'

'It will not be very exciting,' he reminded her.

She tipped her head to the side and took another bite.

'There will be no balls,' he prompted. 'No shopping. Only the neighbours for company.' There would be none of the things that smart, young girls claimed to want. Did she not understand?

She swallowed her toast. 'Do you have a stream for fishing?'

'A very little one,' he admitted. 'The trout are not large. But they are there.'

'And woods?' she pressed, stuffing the last bit of toast into her mouth and licking jam from her fingers.

He watched those fingers for a moment, and the tip of the pink tongue that lapped at them, then shook his head, frustrated to be caught in the same trap that had snared him before.

When he looked up, she was tapping her foot again, chewing furiously and waiting for his answer.

'A wood,' he reminded himself of the subject. 'More of a copse, really. My land is less than ten acres, total. Not all of it has trees. It is not fit for hunting, but good enough for an afternoon stroll. It is just a simple country house and grounds.' It was not as grand as his father's nor likely hers.

'But there are birds,' she said with an approving nod. 'And a meadow? Or is all of it a formal garden?' She made a face as if to say this was not to her liking.

It surprised him. Judging by the parks in London, he'd always assumed that ladies liked nature subdued and in small quantities. 'There are several acres of meadow,' he assured her.

'With wildflowers still in bloom,' she said with a happy sigh.

He remembered her bouquet. 'Yes.'

'And insects, of course,' she said. Once again, she surprised him by making no distasteful grimace. Instead, she seemed to approve of the fact.

'Do you collect them?' he asked.

'You mean dead and on pins?' She shuddered. 'It has always seemed to me a barbarous way to treat one of God's creatures, even small ones.'

'You do not swat flies?' he teased.

She snorted. 'Of course I do, and midges as well. But once I have done, I do not save the corpse under glass as a trophy.'

'Sometimes, for scientific purposes...' he began.

'If one wishes to study an animal, it is far more interesting to watch it go about its daily business. Ants, for example, are fascinating creatures. Have you ever dropped a lump of sugar on an ant hill? There is such joyful industry when they discover it.'

'You find ants to be joyful?' Now he was simply baffled.

She shrugged. 'Perhaps not in the way butterflies seem to be. And they are another type of creature that does not deserve an early memorial beneath glass in the drawing room. Butterflies are nothing but pressed sadness when deprived of flight and energy.'

'But ants...' he reminded her.

'Ants are good little Protestants,' she replied. 'If you look at them under a magnifying glass, you will find they have no faces to smile with. But that does not mean that they are not happy, in their own way. I am sure you would approve of the speed and organisation used to dismantle a sugar lump. It is positively military.'

'Ants do have wars,' he allowed.

She gave him a disappointed shake of her head for even knowing such a thing. 'I prefer to imagine them filling their larders under the ground and contemplating their full stomachs with satisfaction.'

'Happy ants,' he said.

'I suspect you have enough of them on ten acres to keep me busy for many afternoons to come. Now, if you will excuse me, I must get ready to depart.'

She reached past him for one more slice of toast before escaping to her room to call the maid.

George was ready to leave before the horses were fully harnessed. It was not because she cared for Mr Challenger's opinion. Rather, she detested foolish delays. Let no one say the departure was postponed because the lady of the house was searching under the bed for lost ribbons. It also helped that she had begun her packing yesterday morning, after her conversation with Christian.

But that was not a thing she needed to share with her husband. He had been very angry of late and would be even angrier to discover that she had manipulated his rage to her own advantage.

But she was still unsure what she had done that actually bothered him so. She had spent time with his family. Was that not better than associating with strangers? She had played cards at his club. But she had not lost any money, nor had she partaken of any of the truly scandalous activities that had been happening all around them.

And she'd allowed him to kiss her. That could not be wrong, could it? Kissing was something husbands and wives were supposed to do. If how she felt afterwards was any indication, they were very good at doing it. If she was doing it wrong, the least he could do was tell her so, that she might improve.

After breakfast, he seemed to be in a better humour, giving her an approving nod at her speedy preparations. She had selected a small trunk of necessary clothing and saw that it was loaded on to the top of the carriage. The rest would follow with Polly, tomorrow.

When the coachman helped her up into the carriage, she was surprised to see Pootah, the bird, sitting in his brass cage on the seat beside her.

'He is coming with us?' she asked.

'He is your responsibility,' Frederick said, giving her another aloof look. 'Until you can re-train him, he is not fit company for my sisters.'

'You want me to make him talk?' she asked.

'I want you to make him stop,' he corrected. 'The ladies in my family may not understand, but it discommodes me to hear him shouting "whore" each time one of them enters the room.'

'You mean…?'

'Change his name,' Frederick said firmly. 'He must have belonged to a soldier, for he is speaking Portuguese. Some Hindi as well, I think. I will ask Oliver, when he returns to England, but I am not sure that we want to know what else he can say.'

'Oh, dear.' Why was it that, even when she tried to do the right thing, it all went wrong? 'I did not mean anything by it,' she said.

'You could not have known,' he agreed. 'At least, I hope you did not.' Was it her imagination, or was there a faint smile on his face as he turned away from her to look out the window? She could not be sure.

She glanced out of the window as well, watching the city disappear over the horizon. He had assured her that the journey to his house was a short one. Even stopping for lunch, it was less than a day's ride into the country. Despite his early threats of a lack of entertainment, a trip back into town for shopping or society would be an easy one, even without his assistance.

Though she had not yet seen the property, she hoped for the best of both worlds. It would be not quite so remote as her father's land. She would have to forgo some of the long and reckless rambling she had enjoyed growing up. But neither would it be quite so boring in the long winter months when she was forced to keep to the house. He likely had a library with books she had not yet read, and attics and cellars to explore. If the neighbours were not friendly already, she would labour industriously to make them so. When all else failed, there was London.

At the very least, it would keep him out of the way. Since he was still absorbed in the running of his silly club, he could go back into town and enjoy himself, leaving her to her own devices. Perhaps she might not need to take her own rooms after all. She could cede him the town house and remain in the country all year.

When she thought about it, it was a surprise to find the idea so annoying. Though she might insist to herself that she did not want his company any more than she first had, neither did she want to be so easily disposed of. Considering how she'd felt after two days' separation, the idea that he would be spending all his time at Vitium et Virtus, surrounded by naked courtesans and brandy bottles was positively infuriating.

Just then the carriage hit a bump, causing Mr Challenger's coat-tail to shift and dump the contents of its pocket on to the floor. A rectangular leather box slid across the carriage, bumping the toe of her shoe and spilling its contents on to the boards.

Her throat tightened. It was a necklace of amethyst flowers, set in silver. It was so perfect that she had to curl her fingers into a fist to prevent reaching for it. Just because a thing was concealed in her husband's coat did not mean that it was meant for her. More likely, he had bought it for some woman at the club and forgotten to give it away.

She braced herself for whatever denial might come, surprised to find tears pricking at her lashes. She blinked them away, refusing to do so much as reach for a handkerchief lest he notice her distress.

'Well, this is awkward,' he said, confirming her worst fears.

And why was it bothering her so? She was about to be free of him. He had said nothing about plans to remain in Richmond after delivering her there. Once he was gone, she would be completely alone, just as she'd wanted. But now that the moment had arrived, it did not content her. Although she could hardly expect him to love her, it seemed she wanted her husband to like her, at least a little.

She stared down at the jewels, afraid to look up, and took a breath. 'Let us pretend that I did not see it.' Then she closed her eyes and waited for him to return it to his pocket.

Several seconds passed, but he made no effort to retrieve it. 'Will you pretend to be surprised when I give it to you? I shall not believe you, you know. You are not that good an actress.'

'It's for me?' She opened her eyes, wondering if her current surprise was sufficient to satisfy him.

'It's...' He nudged it with his toe, then seemed to realise that it was an inappropriate way to treat a gift and scooped up the box again, arranging the necklace on the satin lining before holding it out to her properly. 'It's a sort of reward, you see. For the speed which you showed in packing.'

'You thought I would do something worthy of a reward?' Perhaps he was not a very good actor, either. The idea that he'd planned a gift to go along with this trip did not seem very likely.

He sighed. 'Not exactly. I saw it this morning, in a shop window. And though I was still very angry with you because of last night, I bought it anyway. I cannot explain the fact.' He sounded as annoyed with himself as he had been with her.

'It is very pretty,' she allowed.

'Would you like me to put it on you?'

Desperately so. But it was not the sort of thing one wore during the day, especially while travelling. The staff at the Richmond house would think their new mistress was quite mad to be arriving in jewels. 'Yes,' she said at last, giving in to the temptation.

He slid to her side of the carriage, bracing his back against the outside wall and forcing himself into what little space was not occupied by her or the birdcage. Then he reached his arms over her head and she felt the weight of the stones settling against her throat as he fastened them.

When he was done, his hands rested on her shoulders for a moment, as if he was not quite ready to remove them. She leaned back, ever so slightly, until her back brushed the lapels of his coat.

The bird in front of her squawked, then announced, *'Boa como o milho.'*

Behind her, her husband laughed.

'What did he say?' she said, worried.

'He thinks you are as good as corn,' he replied, softly. 'It means you are…attractive.' By the way he paused, it likely meant something slightly different than that.

'You really know Portuguese?' She half-turned, interested.

'Enough to train a bird.' He cleared his throat and moved back to his side of the carriage as if relieved that the moment between them had ended.

'What else did you learn when you were in the army?' Since their marriage, she'd made no effort to engage her husband in more than the most superficial conversation. But something had changed. Suddenly, she wanted to know him better.

In exchange for that one simple question, she was rewarded with enough stories to last the rest of the trip. It almost came as a surprise when the carriage pulled up the drive of a large house of grey stone.

She could tell at a glance that it belonged to Frederick Challenger. The shrubs were manicured to such mathematical perfection that she could have balanced a wine glass on the tops of the boxwood hedges. The flower beds were equally well cared for, with not a single weed marring their perfection. Their edges were marked by stone paths free of curves or divots. Everything was as rigidly perfect as he was, down to the last blade of grass.

She held her breath and closed her eyes to shut out the stultifying uniformity of the scene. He had promised a meadow. A stream. A copse of trees. She could cede him an ordered front park and be content with the wilderness in the back. It would be enough.

A servant put down the step for them and Mr Challenger helped her to the ground before turning away and surveying the grounds expectantly. 'Sargent!'

George winced. He'd shouted in a voice loud enough to carry to the stables. This must be how he had sounded on the battlefield, issuing orders that his men would have obeyed from an instinct more deeply rooted than the fear of his anger. It was not a tone that could be ignored.

She looked to the house for the servant who would answer the call. He was probably some former soldier with an infirmity that would have put the man out into the street to beg, were it not for the concern of his former commander. While she could find many faults with her husband, she was utterly confident in his desire to care for those less fortunate. The fact that he'd married her was proof of it.

But instead of the greeting of a trusted retainer, she heard a distant, answering bay. Then the largest bloodhound she had ever seen came galloping around the corner of an outbuilding, long legs pumping furiously in answer to her husband's call.

George waited for the inevitable collision of man and dog and the furious wagging and jumping of an animal rendered ecstatic at his master's homecoming. Instead, as it neared them the four legs seemed to lock and the animal skidded the last few feet, raising a cloud of dust on the sweep as it came to a perfect stop, sitting directly in front of Fred and waiting, still as a statue, to be greeted.

In response, he smiled approval and gave the dog an enthusiastic scratch upon its long floppy ears. 'Good boy. Come meet your mistress.'

There was a brief hand signal from the owner and the dog stepped cautiously to her, sitting at her feet and looking up with large sad eyes.

'If you are at all frightened by dogs, you need have no fear of this one,' Frederick said, with obvious pride. 'Sargent is perfectly trained.'

'Of course he is,' she said weakly. How else would a dog of Major Challenger's be, but as perfectly ordered and obedient as everything else about his life? Everything except for his wife, of course.

Trying not to brood on her own deficiencies, she bent down to talk to the animal. 'How do you do, Sargent?' She offered him her hand, waiting for him to raise a paw.

He looked at her dubiously, as if he had never seen such strange behaviour in his life.

'You do not shake?'

'He has never had a reason to,' Frederick

said, surprised that she would expect it. Apparently, his idea of perfect training did not include anything so whimsical.

'Very well then,' she said to the dog. 'We will have to be much less formal. Then she bent over, took the great head in her two hands and kissed him on the nose.

The dog pulled away in surprise and sneezed as if she had tickled him. Then, he looked up and hesitantly wagged his tail.

'I suppose you have never been kissed before, either.'

By the pinkness of the owner's cheek's, if he had ever relaxed enough to show such extremes of affection, he was not about to admit it.

'Never mind,' she said, still talking to the dog and not the man. 'I like dogs very much. I think we shall get along famously together.' She began to walk towards the house along with her husband, but the dog did not follow.

She turned back to him. 'Well? Come along, then.'

The dog started forward at something that would have been a scamper in a smaller animal, then pulled up short with a whine.

'Sargent?'

Her husband looked back to see what she

was doing. 'Dogs are not allowed in the house,' he said in a tone that brooked no argument.

'Why?' she asked simply. From the wag of his tail, Sargent wanted an answer as well.

'They make a mess,' he said.

'I have had dogs all of my life, both in the house and out. On the whole, they are cleaner than people,' she said.

'But dogs have never been allowed in my house,' he said, significantly.

'And at the altar, you endowed me with all your worldly goods,' she said, smiling. 'That would include both the house and the dog.' She looked down at Sargent. 'Do not listen to him. You are welcome to stay on my half of the house. And you may sleep at the foot of my bed. Come, Sargent.'

The dog gave her one more baffled shake of the head and then wagged his tail and followed her into her new home.

Chapter Fourteen

Mutiny.

After years in the army, Fred had never seen so much as a hint of it from any of the soldiers in his command. But after less than an hour in Georgiana's presence, the loyal Sargent had turned against him.

Not only had the hound come into the house, he had fallen asleep on the sofa in the library. When Fred had scolded him for it, the dog had obeyed and retreated to the rug by the fire. But not before giving him an accusing look to remind him that some members of the family treated him better than this.

Most annoying of all, at bedtime, the dog followed his mistress to the lady's suite, occupying a better place than Fred himself was allowed.

Perhaps his current uneasiness was the

dog's fault. Fred had not thought about the embargo placed upon that one room until he had watched the door shutting on the pair of them. The dog had done nothing to earn a place in her bed. And Fred had given her a necklace.

Such thoughts were unworthy. Wives were not like mistresses. One should not expect rewards in the bedroom for jewellery. Both gifts and affection should be given as a matter of course. Besides, the gift he had given would hardly have turned a courtesan's head. Its silver setting was far too simple to rate more than a peck on the cheek.

And yet, as she had with the plain gold chain, Georgiana had fairly glowed with pleasure when he'd given it to her.

Proof she was easily impressed. Her innocence would extend to the bedroom, as well. If and when he passed that threshold he would be expected to teach her and put her pleasure before his own. After a lifetime of sexual conquest, bedding a virgin would likely be overrated and disappointing.

But he could not stop thinking about doing it.

He thought of her as he lay in his bed, unable to sleep. He thought about her the next morning at breakfast, as they ate on opposite sides of the table and she slipped scraps to the dog under the table. He thought about her later in the morning as he took a ride alone to avoid her. And he thought about her in the afternoon as she took a walk to avoid him. As he dressed for dinner, he caught himself humming the same minuet that she had been whistling to the mynah bird in an attempt to retrain him.

If he was going to leave her here and return to the city, then he should not be bothered by how little time they spent together. If things went according to plan, he would hardly see her at all. Why then did he feel jealous that birds and dogs, and even ants, got more of her attention than he did?

The most enjoyable thing about the country house had always been its solitude. But suddenly, he could find no peace in it. When he was alone, it was as if she was still with him. He could feel her walking his land like a caress on his body and hear her laugh on the breeze that touched his face. The thought of impeding separation made him want to seek her out immediately to convince her that there must be another way.

When they met again at supper, the amethysts glittered above a gown of dove-grey satin. She was different tonight, elegant and silent. When he looked at her, he could not seem to recall what it was about her that had bothered him before, or why he was so eager to escape her.

In the carriage, she had coaxed him into conversation and their time together had passed easily. Since then, she had been silent. Perhaps she was waiting for him to make the next move. When he could no longer stand the silence he attempted conversation. 'Did you enjoy your walk this afternoon?'

She paused with the soup spoon halfway to her mouth, looking at him through the fringe in her lashes as if trying to find a hidden meaning in the words. Then she finished the spoonful, giving herself additional time to find an answer. At last, she spoke. 'I liked it very well, thank you.'

Had he really been holding his breath for this ordinary response?

'Did you take the path to the pond?' It was the nicest view of the house, had she turned to look back.

She nodded. 'There was a family of ducks on the water. Five little ones not yet fledged.

Tomorrow, I will them bring some bread-crumbs from my tea.'

'I will ask the housekeeper to prepare a bag for you on such days as you wish to walk,' he said, searching for something to offer as an olive branch.

'You needn't bother. If I wish for such a thing, I am quite capable of doing it myself,' she replied. There was no rancour in her tone. But it gave him very little to offer her if she was able to take care of herself.

'I did not know if you would be comfortable approaching the servants,' he said, trying to find a way out of the hole he had dug for himself. 'A large staff can be intimidating.'

'I am not the least bit intimidated by servants,' she said, giving him a faintly irritated look. 'I am not some child that needs looking after.'

'I did not think you were,' he said, though it was precisely how he'd viewed her before their marriage. But tonight, it was impossible to see her as anything other than fully grown.

'If you do not think me a child, then please stop treating me as one,' she said in a surprisingly reasonable voice. 'If I had not married you, it would have been someone else.'

'Nash Bowles,' he reminded her.

She shrugged. 'Perhaps. He was not my first offer, only my most persistent. And though I had accepted no one, I expect I would have been married to someone by year's end, and ready to be so, if only to escape my step-mother. Though Marietta does not like me, she has spent years teaching me to take over the management of a home and I am not the least bit frightened of the task. It is what women do, you know, instead of going off to university and starting clubs that decent women should not know about.'

'I see,' he said. His sisters were being trained up much the same way. But he had never thought of Georgiana as capable of anything but chaos.

Now she was looking at him as if he were an idiot. 'You do realise I have been approving the menus of every meal you have eaten, since our wedding day?'

He had not. Food appeared at regular intervals each day he was at home. He had never bothered to ask the housekeeper what was involved in the preparation.

'If you had been home last night, you would have eaten braised veal prepared according to a recipe handed down from my mother.' She paused for emphasis. 'My real mother, not Marietta.'

She had never spoken of her mother. But by the loneliness in her voice, now, she had loved and been loved in return. Had she chosen the meal to ease homesickness? Or had she been trying to send him a message with it? If she had, he had ignored it by staying at the club. 'I am sorry I missed it,' he said, surprised to find that he was. 'You must make it again for me some time.'

She smiled and nodded. 'As you wish. Be sure to inform me of the day of your departure, so I might plan accordingly.'

'My departure?'

'I assume you are planning to go back to London and abandon me here so I will not be able to cause more trouble,' she said. 'The only thing I do not know is the date you are leaving.'

Perhaps she was right when she claimed he'd treated her as a child. He had never thought that she would understand the meaning of this trip, much less plan any part of her day according to his presence or absence. He'd meant to leave as soon as he had assured himself she had adjusted to her new surroundings. Apparently, that had already happened. He could go tomorrow morning, if he wished.

'You do have plans, do you not?' Now, she was patiently waiting for him to admit the truth.

'Nothing specific,' he said, baffled by his own words. If this was a contest, he had won it by removing her from all the things that might cause him embarrassment. She had not fought the removal to Richmond. She was not planning to argue with his departure. He was free to do as he liked, just as he had been before marriage. And yet...

He shook his head again. 'I thought... think... I... I think I will stay for a few days. Perhaps a week, or two. London gets so oppressively hot in July. And there is much about the house here that needs tending to.' He had not seen Sargent in some time, either. It was hardly fair to the dog to pat him on the head and get immediately back on his horse. The more he thought of it, the more foolish it seemed to ride out immediately just to avoid a woman who had not been bothering him in anyway.

She smiled and nodded. 'Mrs Pimm and I shall plan the menus only a few days in advance. You have but to inform me, should you change your mind.'

'It will not upset you to have me here?' he asked. A voice in the back of his mind argued that it did not really matter if it did upset her. It was his job to make the decisions and hers to defer. But the fledgling diplomat in him countered that she was more likely to be agreeable if he did not actively try to provoke her.

'Upset me.' She thought for a moment. 'I hardly know you well enough to be upset by your behaviour. As far as I can tell, you do not do very much of anything.'

'I do not *do* things?' Did she think him idle? Or useless in some way?

She shrugged, as if annoyed that he would take offence. 'You run the club, of course. But for once, let us not speak of it. Beyond that?' She shrugged again. 'I do not shadow your every step to see how you occupy yourself. You have spent a fair amount of your time attempting to organise me, of course.'

When he thought back over the last week, he had expended a surprising amount of mental and physical energy trying and failing to gain her obedience. He had not thought it would be easier to command a battalion than a single woman.

'I do not enjoy your constant criticism,' she added.

'I noticed,' he said, trying not to smile.

'But after living with Marietta for seven years, I am inured to such things.' She sighed.

'You do not like her,' he said, stating the obvious.

'It does not matter,' she replied. 'I thought, at first, there might be some way to get rid of her. But I was a child then and did not understand that was not how marriage worked.' She frowned. 'I could not fathom that the woman brought into the house to mother me would not want to, or that it might be possible for my father to love someone who did not love me.'

'I notice you write to your father often,' he said. He had seen her sitting down with pen and paper on several occasions and noted the regular letters in the outgoing post. 'What have you heard from him in return?' But he knew the answer to that, for he had seen nothing from him in the incoming mail.

'I suspect he has been too busy for letter writing. Not everyone is as regular a correspondent as I am.' She touched a napkin to her lips, as if signalling the end of the meal might be some distraction. 'Shall I ring for coffee, or would you prefer to take port?'

She was preparing to retreat to the parlour and leave him alone to have a glass and smoke in peace. And what would she do? Likely, she would write a letter to a man who showed no sign of answering. Fred held up a hand. 'It seems rather a silly custom for you to withdraw when there are just the two of us here. Why don't we go to the library? There is something there that might interest you.'

They rose from the table and she followed him down the hall, with Sargent walking between them.

What he was about to do was probably a mistake. It was a ridiculous thing to give to any woman. He need not have bothered to think of it as a gift. He could have simply referred her to the shelf in the library where it sat. Though he was normally quite clueless about such things as the feelings of others, he was not so big an idiot that he could not sense the heaviness in the air around his normally spirited wife.

She had a right to be melancholy. He had begun the day by driving her to into the country with the intent of abandoning her there like an unwanted animal, then bought her off with a cheap trinket. He'd demonstrated that he had no idea of her knowledge or ability when it came to running a house. He had accidentally commented on the fact that the father she clearly loved had not taken the time to write even a single line of congratulations to her after the marriage.

And though he had given her the loyalty of his favourite dog, he hardly deserved credit for it. He had not intended that to happen. Nor could he look at the chronically depressed expression on Sargent's floppy face and tell himself that this was the sort of dog one should offer to a pretty young girl who was probably near to tears herself.

When they arrived in the library, she poured his glass of port as he searched the shelves for the book he thought she would enjoy. As he glanced back at her, she tipped her head to the side as she so often did when intrigued. But this time she bit her lip as if actively trying not to appear too eager for his attention.

It made him all the more eager to impress her. He held out the book to her.

'*The Naturalist's and Traveller's Compan-*

ion,' she read, stroking the cover and taking it from him.

'It is really intended for explorers,' he said. 'I know that you do not approve of capturing and killing specimens for no reason, but the illustrations are interesting. And there is much that you might find useful about the pressing of flowers and taking rubbings from coins and monuments. And so forth,' he added, feeling rather lame about the whole thing.

'And I expect you read it, as a boy?' she said. The corners of her mouth turned up just a little and the hooded gaze that accompanied her half-smile held fondness, curiosity, and something else he could not quite name.

Whatever it was, his body recognised it immediately. The last time he'd felt something similar, he'd probably been reading the very same book, ready to share the interesting illustrations, only to look at the girl next to him and see that there were things in the world infinitely more exciting than a collection of brightly coloured beetles.

He cleared his throat, and tried to focus on the book. 'As a boy, yes, I studied it religiously. Most lads plan to go on a great adventure at some point in their life. Mine was on the Peninsula, of course. And Belgium. But at one point, my ambitions were far more tame. Exploration of the Congo.'

She made that face again, the frustrated grimace she often wore when coming up against one of the strictures of womanhood. 'When I was that age, my governess was dead set on my learning to draw flowers without actually learning anything about them. My watercolours are dreadful. But I did do a pastel of Anne Bonny the pirate. She was standing on the severed heads of her enemies with a raised sword dripping blood.'

'You must have been quite proud of it,' he said.

'Miss Soames showed it to Marietta. They made me burn it. I had to spend the next six months embroidering samplers with uplifting verses.'

'Horrifying,' he replied.

'The picture or the samplers?' she asked.

'Both, I should think. I would rather have framed and hung the pastel than received any number of moralising cushions or candle screens.'

At this, she smiled and it was as if she had never done so before. He had seen the expression directed at others and been jealous of their luck. When she smiled at him, he knew it was with mockery or insincerity. At worst, it was a masking expression used to hide her annoyance at whatever he had just said or done. At best, she seemed to mute any real joy she felt, as if convinced that he would only spoil it if he knew her to be happy about something.

But right now, she was smiling at him.

He blinked slowly, trying to focus on the book she was holding and not the graceful curve of her shoulder as it dipped into the bodice of the gown, the fabric of which he knew was hiding a pair of stunning breasts that should be pressed into the pillows on his bed and not the grass next to an anthill.

'Be careful what you wish for, Mr Challenger,' she said, and for a moment, he was sure she'd read his thoughts. Then she continued. 'I've a mind to take up sketching again. Then I will reproduce my lost work and insist you hang it in pride of place over your desk.'

'I will consider it an honour, madam,' he said. And what a relief it would be if that was the most shocking thing in his future.

Chapter Fifteen

As George laid in bed that night, she could not help thinking that it had been a delightful evening. She would not have thought it possible, but she had enjoyed talking with her husband even more than the dancing and kissing at the ball. Tonight, he had been the one to instigate the conversation. And though they had talked for almost two hours, she could not remember a single criticism in the whole time.

He had shared a favourite book with her. Even though she had her own copy and knew it as well or better than he did, she had read it again for his sake.

As she had done so, he had been staring at her. Her body grew warm at the memory of his gaze and she pushed the bedcover off, causing Sargent to groan in his sleep. She could not blame him. The memory of those dark eyes fixed on her would make sleep impossible.

He had not been angry. There had been no reason for it. But the intensity was much more than casual interest. Had he wanted to kiss her again? Then why had he not done so? It was not as if they needed to fear discovery. They were in their own home. The servants would think it quite normal should one of them accidentally catch newlyweds kissing in a public room. If the idea bothered him, he could have suggested that they go to bed. Even now, she could open the connecting door between their rooms.

And then what would happen? Somehow, when she imagined the scene, she could not see beyond the first kiss. He would hold her. He would kiss her. Then, suddenly, they would be unclothed, like the people in the paintings at Vitium et Virtus.

She frowned. It was not a very accurate imagining, if that happened. There was no fumbling with buttons or laces, no calls for a maid to undo a troublesome knot, or requests to wait, just a moment, while one put shirt studs or eardrops on the dresser where they would not be lost.

Instead, one moment they were clothed and

the next they were not, as if there was some reason to hurry. Once her clothes were off, she would know exactly what to do that would make him happiest, for he would be smiling as he had tonight instead of frowning like he usually did. He would call her his beautiful love and not a troublesome nuisance.

She remembered him that first night, disciplined yet angry, waving a cat-o'-nine-tails and driving the lechers away from her. She had never seen a man so fierce, so powerful, and so attractive. The libertine residing just beneath the carefully civilised veneer he presented intrigued her. Before he had rescued her from Sir Nash and been forced into a proposal, he had bought her. What would he have done had the auction been in earnest?

She stretched in bed, imagining herself at the mercy of Frederick Challenger.

He would touch her breasts, which somehow seemed to think and feel on their own at times like this. They did not precisely itch, but they were so eager to be touched that she had to clutch the bedsheets to keep herself from rubbing her nipples.

There were other places that wanted touching as well. And that, she was pretty sure, had to do with the act of procreation. One did not grow up in the country without learning a few facts about reproduction. She had learned far too much of horses until the grooms had shooed her away from the stallions and mares.

But it could not be the same with people. For one thing, gentleman could not manage to wear such tight pants, if they were anything like horses. And mares did not seem to enjoy what happened very much. There was a lot of stomping and snapping.

But if what humans did was unpleasant, then surely she would have heard something about it. Women complained about childbirth, but not the act that caused it. And all the women in the paintings at Vitium et Virtus had seemed happy enough, as had the female guests she had seen leading gentlemen up the stairs.

When the moment came for her, if it ever did, she prayed that she would know what to do. Frederick would not think her bothersome or stupid. He would think she was wonderful and would tell her so repeatedly. Then they would lie together in the bed, still naked, and there would be more kissing and no arguing at all until after they got up.

Because, no matter how good it might be in

bed, and how good it had been tonight, she was sure there would still be arguing. Perhaps there was something that she could do that would render him not quite so totally unreasonable. But short of a blow to the head that left him permanently dazed, she could not think of what it might be.

At supper, he had claimed that he had no immediate plans to return to London. But even if he came to her bed, he would go eventually, back to the club he had forbidden her to enter. She had not seen him do anything particularly scandalous, when she had been there. But she could not imagine him forgoing the pleasures that he was not sharing with his wife.

He would be there and she would be miles away, wondering about him. She would be tossing in bed as she was tonight, her skin hot, her body tingling, wanting whatever it was that women got when their husbands thought of them as a wife and not an inconvenience.

She could not stand the thought of it any more. To be so near to him but still alone was agony. She slid out of bed and, without bothering to grab a wrap or slippers, slipped out of her bedroom, down the stairs, and out of the front door of the house.

She ran through the yard, feeling the cool grass between her toes. It was a warm night. The moon was full and so bright that it was almost like walking in daylight, but there was not enough breeze to dry the perspiration that made her nightgown cling uncomfortably to her body. She paused for a moment, weighing the wisdom of her plan against how pleasant it might be. Then she turned her steps toward the pond.

It was not really an escape, she reminded herself. She was still on the property. But with each step she took she felt more peaceful than she had since the kiss on the balcony. It was not as if she wanted to get away from him. No matter how hard it was, it was better than being married to Nash Bowles. But that did not make this marriage right.

Her parents had been happy together. But more than that. She had seen the love in them when they had looked into each other's eyes. It had been something she'd expected, when she had begun to search for a husband. But as she had watched other girls accept offers with little more than lukewarm affection, she had begun to see just how rare a thing such shared feelings must be. To find that she was falling in love with Frederick Challenger, of all people...

Perhaps it was not love at all. Maybe it was only lust. She had never felt that before. Perhaps the two were indistinguishable from each other. It was perfectly normal to be attracted to a handsome man. But it would be foolish to fall in love with a man who'd spent most of their acquaintance looking at her as though she was a broken toy that needed to be fixed.

She reached the edge of the pond and bent over it, cupping her hands and scooping up the clear dark water and splashing it on to her heated face.

She was not in love. If her feelings were more than temporary infatuation, she would begin to care that they were not reciprocated. Then, she would begin trying to follow his rules and trying to act normal to please him. Since she had no idea what normal was, she would likely fail. Even if she succeeded, there was no proof that it would be enough to win his heart. It was just as likely that he would raise the bar once she had reached it and become even more strict.

She dipped a bare toe into the water, watching the silver trail of tiny waves in the moonlight. It was some consolation that, if she had to be alone, it was at least a beautiful evening. The song of night birds was loud in the still air. The water at her feet was as warm as a bath.

Did she dare to swim in it? Frederick had promised her that the land around his home would be as much hers as it was his. What was to prevent her from enjoying it? Without another thought she stripped her nightgown over her head and spread it on a bush to keep it from the damp grass. Then, she waded into the water and dived for the centre.

This was what she had needed. Her worries seemed to melt away with the water. When she broke the surface, the drops clinging to her arms were as bright as diamonds. She splashed in front of her, watching the ripples and laughing softly at the wonder of it all. Perhaps it would not be so bad to be alone if she could have more nights like this.

With a few easy strokes, she was back to the side again and threw herself down on the mossy bank to let the air dry her skin and hair before returning to the house. She closed her eyes and watched the silver light still patterning the inside of her eyelids.

Suddenly, everything went dark.

She opened them, expecting to see a cloud on the face of the moon. Instead, the dark silhouette of a man was blocking the light. She gasped and reached for something to cover herself, then stopped. It was far too late to worry about such things, even if she'd had a robe within reach.

'What the devil are you doing?' Her husband's voice brought the first chill to the night air.

'I should think that was obvious,' she replied, trying to keep the fear from her reply. How long had he been watching her? It did not matter, for he could see her now, lying at his feet as naked as a pagan offering.

But he did not appear to be moved by the sight of her. 'If you wished to swim, we could have gone to Bath for the waters. Or you could have gone to Brighton and dressed appropriately for it.'

'I could have dressed to swim,' she said, squinting up to try to decipher the expression on his face. There was no point in bothering, for it was most certainly disapproval. 'Have you ever tried to swim in the costumes allowed to women, on such rare occasions that we are encouraged into the water?'

The silence of his response was answer enough.

'Nor have you been carted into the water like freight in a bathing machine,' she said. 'It makes no sense to be wheeled into the deep and hauled back again, just to avoid getting mud between one's toes.'

'If you find the process of going for a lady-like sea bath so objectionable, you should refrain from the water altogether.' There was a curious quality to his voice now, as if he was barely maintaining control of something.

'But I like to swim,' she said. 'It is quite liberating.' She made an expansive gesture, only to remember that when one was still totally nude, it did not do to debate the merits of athletics.

'You are quite liberated enough for one evening, I think,' he said, snatching her nightgown from its branch and tossing it to her.

'And, as usual, you are more constricted than I thought it was possible for a man to be,' she said, scrambling to her feet and clutching the fabric between her hands.

'Constricted?' His face was still in shadow, but she could imagine the look of anger that must be there. 'I've a good mind to show you what happens when constraints are removed.'

'I wish you would. Then perhaps I would not think I had married an unbearable prig.'

Words failed him. He responded with a feral growl and closed the distance between them with a single step, yanking the nightgown from her hands and casting it aside. Then, he seized her, pulling her to him and smothering her mouth with a ferocious kiss.

There was something in it beyond passion and beyond need. His mouth was open on hers, his tongue questing along the seam in her closed lips. She refused to open them for him, angry that he could forget the kindnesses of a few hours past and return to his old ways the first time she disappointed him.

His hands squeezed her bare bottom to elicit a gasp that gave him free access to her mouth. He thrust his tongue into it, retreated and repeated. It moved in her mouth, a low commanding pulse, as if he could reset the beating of her heart to the rhythm of his choosing.

He broke away, messaging the flesh beneath his hands in the same slow tempo. 'I am an insufferable prig named Frederick. Say my name. You say it often enough when we are in public and you do not have to mean it.'

Of course she meant it. It was as if he was

claiming that she did not know how a noun worked, which was utter nonsense.

'Say it,' he repeated, and moved a hand between them to squeeze one of her bare breasts.

'Frederick,' she gasped, surprised at the longing in her own voice.

'Georgiana,' he answered, as if speaking her name was some kind of reward. The slow massage continued, one hand pinching her nipple, the other rocking her hips against the wool of his breeches, moulding them to the hard bulge pulsing behind the flap. 'You commented before on the paintings decorating the walls of Vitium et Virtus. How closely did you look at them?'

She shook her head, afraid to admit or deny lest he decide to punish her by sending her back to the house alone.

'It does not matter. I will explain them to you, now.' His voice was low, silky. Not precisely menacing, but definitely dangerous. And yet, it did not frighten her.

'There is a particularly nice oil of a nymph surprised while bathing,' he said. 'This nymph stripped bare in the moonlight in a pond where a gentleman might look out of his bedroom window and see her. And what do you suppose he did to her?'

She did not know. But she was sure that she was about to find out.

'The sight of her made his cock hard.' He stepped away from her long enough to capture one of the hands that were resting at her sides, pressing it against his breeches.

Then he slipped his hand between her legs, his fingers teasing, stroking her opening with a single fingertip. 'And then he put it deep inside of her.' Slowly, his finger slid into her body, just as he described.

The touch left her so weak that she clung to his shirtfront for support. In doing so, her own hands grazed the sides of her naked breasts. The sudden shock of pleasure she felt was nothing like the gentle tingling she'd imagined. She had never known that it was possible to feel so much. Every inch of her skin was awake to him.

As it had been on the night at the club, he had not bothered with cravat or waistcoat. There was only the linen of his shirt separating them. But this time, it was damp from the water that had been on her body and clinging to his chest. She could feel the heat of him and the angry beat of his heart next to her as his finger moved in and out.

Then it was gone, sliding forward, spreading

wetness to another, even more sensitive spot. As he toyed with her, he kissed her again, his tongue back in her mouth. She fought against it, wanting to be free to tell him how good this was, to scream in pleasure into the night sky.

But he refused to let her go, as if he would swallow the joy that burst from her as wave after wave of shudders racked her body. Her knees trembled and the place he had touched her throbbed with need for the thing he had promised. When he released her, she fell to her knees before him, no longer able to support her own weight.

He stood quiet, staring down at her for a moment. When he spoke, his words were like a tongue licking her skin. 'You do not know what you are offering, do you, my sweet? Perhaps some day I will show you. For now, I think I shall have you in a way that is as conventional as you accuse me of being.'

He stripped the shirt over his head and dropped it in the grass beside her nightgown. Then he undid the flap of his breeches and let his manhood spring free.

She stared at it for a moment, dazed by the nearness of it. Then he dropped to his knees as well and pushed her gently backwards, down into the moss of the bank. He straddled her waist and ran his palms down her body to cup her breasts again. He was saying something, but for a moment she could not hear. She was too lost in the feeling of his thumbs pressing against her nipples, drawing slow circles around them, pinching them, almost to the point of pain, and soothing them with featherlight touches.

'...teased me long enough.' His words were almost loud enough to overcome the pounding of the blood in her ears. 'If you mean to cavort naked on the lawn, then do not claim to be surprised by what is about to occur.'

But she was surprised. The last few moments had been full of revelations. She expected the next few moments would be nothing short of miraculous.

He leaned forward to kiss her breasts, taking them into his mouth just as he had drawn her tongue into it when she had tried to cry out. She clutched at his head, twining her fingers in his hair, and gave up to the feeling with a sigh.

Then it occurred to her that she could touch him just as he had touched her. She reached down, searching for the part of him that was straining towards her, circling it with her hands, and sliding up the length of it to cover the wet tip.

'Dear God!' He released her breasts and sat straight up as if his entire body had spasmed in shock, just as hers had done earlier.

'Am I doing this right?' she asked breathlessly, stroking him again, spreading the wetness down the length of him.

'Vixen.' His hands were clutching at the moss as he took a slow sucking breath, as if fighting for control. Then he covered her hands with his own and showed her how to touch him, before reaching out again and covering her breasts, rubbing the nipples with his thumbs. 'It is right. But it is wrong as well. I want more from you.' One hand slid between her legs and the fingers settled inside of her, matching the rhythm of her strokes. 'I want this from you.'

'Yes,' she whispered, tightening her grip on him, ever so slightly, and increasing the speed of her strokes.

He dipped his head forward and his teeth grazed the side of her neck, just as the stallion had done to the mare. His fingers thrust harder into her, deeper. 'It will hurt the first time. But not after that.'

Which meant they would do it more than once. At the thought of it, the feeling was taking her again, making her wonder why people did anything but this. 'Do it,' she said. 'Quickly.'

'Soon,' he answered, pushing her legs apart with his knees and spreading her wide with his fingers. The last few thrusts with his hand were rough, possessive. Then he seized her hands and pulled them away from him. 'Touch yourself,' he ordered, and she had never been so eager to obey.

She clutched her own breasts, squeezing them between her fingers, as he grabbed her hips and entered her with one quick thrust.

It hurt.

She pinched herself as a distraction, surprised to find that she liked the pain. He thrust again. And again. And then, suddenly, he arched his back and seemed to pour himself into her before sagging back, limp.

'That was all?' she said, surprised.

'Because you touched me,' he said, sounding smug. Then he rolled them so that he was lying under her. 'Did you finish?'

'Finish what?' she asked, breathless.

He made a noise somewhere between a sigh

and a laugh. 'If you have to ask, then the answer is no. Sit up. I want to see your face when it happens.' His hands were on her shoulders, pushing her up so she could sit, straddling his body.

She looked down at him, confused by the demand, until he took one of her hands and pressed it to the place where they were still joined, tracing a spot with his own fingers before dragging her knuckles over it.

Oh.

He was right. There was something left unfinished inside her, like a bubble ready to burst.

'You will be even more beautiful when you come,' he whispered, moving her own hand against her. 'And if I am inside you, I can feel the muscles of your body hugging mine.'

'Oh.' She'd said it aloud this time, unable to stop the sound.

'When we make love, I want to know that you have been pleased to the point of exhaustion. It is your right to demand this from me.'

'Oh,' she said again, but this time it sounded like a moan. And she did not want to demand, so much as she wanted to beg for him to continue what he was doing.

'Make me touch you,' he said, stroking the still-tender place where his body disappeared into hers. 'Or touch yourself and let me watch. The sight of your climax will make me hard.'

'Ah.' It was as it had been before, but even better. She could not control the shaking of her body, or the sounds coming from her mouth. This was what she had been missing, what she had wanted, all along. And as he had promised, she could feel him again, swelling to fill her.

Slowly, the ecstasy subsided to pleasure, like a banked fire that could spring to life at any moment. In the corner of her eye, a shaft of moonlight revealed the house and its rows of darkened windows where anyone might have been watching. 'What have we done?' she said, in a whisper and tried to pull away.

'What we should have done from the first night,' he said with a satisfied smile, holding her tight. 'If I had known it was going to be like this, I'd have let you seduce me ages ago.'

'I seduced you?' Since she'd had no idea what she was doing, it seemed unlikely.

'With every word, every gesture, every look, from the first moment we met,' he said.

'We should probably not have done it in the

garden, though,' she said glancing back at the house again.

He laughed softly under her. 'It is too late to agree with me now.'

'We had best go inside,' she said. But if she was honest, she did not want to. The slight movements of his body under hers hinted at things yet to explore.

'When I have finished with you, Wife,' he said. He had called her wife with a possessive pleasure that sent another thrill through her body. This was followed by a buck of his hips, as if he was urging her to movement.

'What if someone sees?' she said, tightening on him and feeling the beginning of another tremor.

He grabbed her by the waist and rolled until she was stretched out beneath him, receiving another thrust of his hips.

'Then let them look.'

And then, nothing mattered for quite some time.

Chapter Sixteen

The next morning, George removed a piece of grass from her hair, laying it carefully on the bedside table lined up with others she had found. What would Polly think when she found the sheets damp and littered with leaves?

Probably the same thing Frederick's valet thought, as his master tried to whistle during his morning shave. The house had gone mad. But quite happily so, George thought, rolling out of the bed and reaching for her nightgown.

Then she laughed. It was quite possible that it was still draped over a bush by the side of the pond. When they had returned to the house, she had been wearing Frederick's shirt, which had come practically to her knees. He had been bare chested, holding up his breeches with one hand and carrying his boots in the other.

But he had been grinning like a fool, as if it was not the least bit out of character to forget all propriety and make love in the garden.

He stood in her doorway, now, staring at her as her maid dressed her hair. 'Good morning, Wife.' He looked very satisfied with himself, as if it was their activity last night that had made her such and not a proper church ceremony.

'You must call me by my name, if you want to get my attention,' she said, unable to resist scolding him, if only in play.

'Georgiana,' he said, as if the one word was every wonderful thing he could think of in the world.

'Thank you,' she said. Then added, 'Frederick.' It did not seem to have the right tone, to fully convey how she felt, after last night. She tried again. 'Frederick.'

I love you.

They had not actually said the words to each other as yet. Not even in the heat of passion had that occurred. But by the way he grinned at the sound of it, she was sure he understood.

He blew a kiss to her reflection in the mirror. Had she really called him a prig last night?

Because she could not imagine anything more foolish and fond than the gesture he had just made.

When they met in the breakfast room, he was still smiling. He rose as she entered, not out of standard courtesy, but for the opportunity to kiss her on the cheek before she sat. Then he returned to his seat, looking both smug and happy. 'Did you rest well, my dear?'

'You know I did not,' she said, trying not to laugh.

'I suppose this means that we must adjust the terms of our truce,' he said.

After the previous night, she had forgotten that their arrangement was supposed to be temporary. 'If you wish to,' she said, cautiously.

'It seems foolish for us to only pretend to be happy with each other for the sake of propriety, when we have found at least one thing we both enjoy,' he said.

What they'd shared had been wonderful. But she wondered if it was enough. 'There is still much we do not agree on,' she reminded him.

'Your capricious nature,' he said.

'And your inflexibility,' she countered.

He sighed and gave a half-hearted nod. 'I will admit that my rigidity can be a fault. But I believe a higher level of self-control is necessary to prevent myself from giving in to the excesses of which my family is guilty.'

'You fear you will become like your father or brother?' She looked at him in surprise. For despite the things she had heard about his past, she saw nothing that led her to believe he was a rake. 'Do you drink to excess?'

'Occasionally,' he admitted. 'But then, what man does not?'

'True,' she agreed. 'But when you are at your worst, do you feel you are a slave to the bottle?'

'Not at all.'

'And have you ever duelled?'

He shook his head.

'Not even in your youth?'

'When I give offence, I apologise. And if I am offended? I have seen far too much killing to desire to do harm to someone over a petty slight.'

'Do you lack moderation in your spending? Are you a dandy? Are you in debt? An intemperate gambler?'

'No, no, and no,' he said, and seemed surprised at the ease in the denials.

'And despite what you fear of me, I am not unchaste or immoderate in dress or diet,' she said.

'I never thought you unchaste,' he said hurriedly.

No. He'd merely thought her foolish. But that might change with time. And for now, she must do her best to prove him wrong.

'Then what, precisely, are you convinced you need to guard against?'

He paused, as if trying to find the words. 'Before I joined the army, there was a night where I came close to committing a sin more grave than any done by the rest of my family.' He paused again. He looked like a man on the verge of confession.

She held up a hand. 'You do not have to tell me, you know. Whatever it was, it is in the past.'

'That is true,' he agreed, though he did not seem to believe it.

'And very nearly doing something is not the same as doing it,' she reminded him. 'Did you join the army to prevent further temptation?'

His silence to this was answer enough.

'If you have not succumbed to temptation since returning to London, then your character has improved,' she said. 'But you have become overly cautious about small infractions because you have been living in fear.'

'I fear nothing,' he said without hesitation.

'No man,' she agreed. 'I suspect there is no physical threat you could not face without blinking. But you are afraid of becoming as careless as the rest of your family. If you have not done so by now, despite the opportunities presented at Vitium et Virtus, I think you are probably safe from precipitous changes in character.'

He was staring at her in surprise, as if the idea had never occurred to him that he was not wicked to the core.

She used his silence to press her advantage. 'While I doubt I will ever be as conventional as you wish for me to be, I promise that I will not intentionally behave in a way that would damage your reputation.'

'Excellent.' He agreed almost too quickly. 'Now that we are in agreement we will live together as ordinary husbands and wives do. Let us have no more talk of separate lives or houses. From now on, we will be happy together.' He stood up and walked to her side of the table to kiss her on the top of her head, just as she did to Sargent, when he as being particularly good.

* * *

Perhaps living in London had been the problem all along. They should have come to the country right after the wedding. It seemed to Fred that his wife's behaviour had changed for the better the moment he had suggested the trip.

He had assumed she would be like all other women of his experience, in constant need of social stimulation. But it seemed she would rather be in the garden or galloping in the woods, than parading on Rotten Row, or bundling herbs in the still room instead of shopping for ribbons.

But if he was honest, he felt the same. He thanked God often that he had not been saddled with a seat in Parliament, talking about doing things rather than picking up a sword and wading into battle. Nor was he eager to take on the minutiae of bookkeeping at Vitium et Virtus as Jake had done.

She had pleased him in other ways as well. He had assumed there would be difficulties because of her youth and inexperience, but she ran the house as efficiently as an army quartermaster. She had no trouble understanding what was expected of her and was quick to learn any skills that she lacked.

And in one aspect of marriage, they suited perfectly. Since the night by the pond, she had risen from his bed each morning, hair tousled by the vigour of their lovemaking, throat reddened by the force of his kisses. This morning, she'd cast a look at him over her shoulder as if daring him to take her again.

And he had. He had scrambled from the bed, grabbed her by the waist, and dragged her back to the mattress, entering her and spending like a green boy on his first time. Rather than being shocked at the briefness of the encounter, she had laughed at him, trailing a finger down his chest and teasing herself to orgasm. Then she had taken him in hand and brought him back to life so they might begin again, but slower.

Perhaps his friends were right and he had more in common with Georgiana than he'd first thought. He had not felt so alive in years.

But pleasant though it might be, he could not devote the whole of his waking life to her. He had promised his friends he would not walk away from his role at the club. If the masquerade planned for the following evening was to run smoothly, it would be necessary for him to attend. And though he had no intention of allowing his wife to set his comings and goings, he could not just disappear without notice.

Since she made a habit of long walks, he had to search half the property to find her. Eventually he was drawn to the lower meadow by the sound of another of her one-sided conversations with Sargent.

'We could have more fun together if you had a ball, or a rag to pull on, or any other plaything. You poor dog.'

Of course, the dog had no idea what she was saying. But he was wagging his tail as if he had never met a more wonderful person in his life and would gladly learn English if it would make her happy.

'How about a stick?' she suggested. She searched around for a possibility. But as usual, the gardeners had done such a good job of clearing the brush and there was none to be had.

Then, as he watched, she spied a nearby apple tree. Despite her skirts, she managed to clamber high enough up the trunk to grab a fruit off one of the lower branches. She held it out to show him. 'You mustn't eat this, for it is far too green. It will give you a bellyache.

But you are trained as a hunter, are you not? I am sure your mouth is so gentle that you will not even leave a mark.'

The dog sat at her feet, staring at her face intently as if trying to comprehend this torrent of unfamiliar words.

She tossed the apple to him. 'Catch.'

It bounced off his nose, earning her an indignant look that asked why, if she claimed to love him, she had suddenly taken to throwing fruit.

'You are supposed to catch it,' she said patiently. 'Then give it to me and I will toss it again.'

'You need to give him a better reason than that.' Fred could not help interrupting, if only to save the dignity of his dog.

'He needs a reason to play?' she said, shaking her head in amazement. Perhaps it was amazing to her. It sometimes seemed that his new wife was not so much an ordinary woman, but an elemental spirit of joy. Now, she was staring not at the dog, but at him. 'What a sad life he must have led, before I arrived.'

'He did well enough,' Fred replied, suddenly unsure.

'Did he really?' That steady gaze was like

the touch of a surgeon, probing gently at an old wound.

'He was satisfied with order, and quiet, and following the commands that were given to him,' Fred said, wondering why that sounded like such cold comfort.

'But was he happy?' she insisted.

He had been as happy as a dog could expect to be. They had both been. Comfort came with predictability and reliability. The distance between unfettered joy and profound regret was too close to risk.

But Georgiana had been the very opposite of such staid emotions. She was like a Russian doll, a nested series of surprises, each more pleasant than the last. A month ago, he'd had no reason to be dissatisfied with his life. But it paled in comparison to what he felt today, when he looked at the woman beside him. 'He was content,' he admitted at last, looking away from her to the dog at their feet. 'But he was not happy. He did not know that there could be another way.'

'Then it is good that I came here,' she said. 'For I would wish him to be as happy as I am, now that I am with you.'

For some reason, her happiness seemed to

increase his own. His heart ached in his chest like an unused muscle forced to stretch after years without use. To hide his confusion, he scooped the apple from the ground and sent it bouncing into the field. Then he looked at the dog and said, 'Fetch.'

Just as he had been trained to do, the dog gave one quick wag of his tail and was off into the grass, searching for his prize. In only a few moments, he was back, the apple held carefully in his mouth. He dropped it at the feet of his master and sat, patiently, waiting for a response.

'Good boy.' Georgiana smiled at the dog, patting him. Then she cast a sidelong look up at Fred that hinted there might be rewards for him as well.

He looked back to Sargent, blushing. 'Again?'

There was another wag of the tail.

He handed the apple to Georgiana, prepared to teach her how to throw.

She wound up and let loose with a pitch worthy of a world-class bowler. 'Fetch, Sargent.'

He laughed, amazed by her once more. 'You have played cricket.'

'I suppose it is too late to deny it,' she said, straightening her skirts.

'I don't know why I am surprised,' he said, shaking his head. 'Who taught you?'

'The stable boys on my father's land,' she said, as unrepentant as ever.

'And I suppose they also taught you to climb trees,' he said.

'And play drumhead,' she agreed. 'My father was the one that taught me to handle a carriage. Because it was more ladylike than riding astride.'

'There were no little girls in the household?' he asked.

'Not a one. Until Marietta arrived, I was free of feminine influence and happy to be so.'

'And after?' he asked.

'Not content,' she said simply. 'I do not do as well with order as you and Sargent.'

'I noticed,' he said, smiling.

Sargent returned with the apple, looking from one to the other of them before dropping it at Georgiana's feet. She picked it up and prepared to throw again. Then she paused. 'Are you about to tell me that it is improper for a lady to play games meant for boys?'

'I suppose I might, if you mean to hoist up

your skirts and play a game by the Serpentine,' he said. 'But I see no reason you cannot throw a ball for the dog.'

She nodded. 'Then I will show you what it looks like when I am not holding back to protect your delicate male sensibilities.' She threw it again, even farther than before.

Fred whistled in amazement. 'It is a shame we did not have you at Eton.'

'You would not have known what to do with a girl there.'

He slipped a hand around her waist and dragged her to the ground. 'But I know what to do with one now.'

'We are in a field in broad daylight,' she reminded him with a wicked grin. 'Anyone might walk by.'

They were a half mile from the nearest path and lying in grass so deep the foxtails were waving over their heads. By the sound of his distant baying, even Sargent had found something more interesting to do than bother them. All the same, Fred returned her smile as he tossed up her skirts. 'Then I'd best be quick about it.'

'About what?' she said, gasping as his lips touched the inside of her thigh.

'Another lesson in your education,' he said, continuing to kiss his way upward. 'If you happened to look at the ceiling while you played cards, what I am about to do to you what was happening to the Roman girl painted directly over your head.'

Chapter Seventeen

'Oh, dear.'

He was kissing his way up the inside of her leg until his mouth settled on the place that gave her the most pleasure. He grazed the little bud of sin with his teeth before swirling his tongue around it, then dipped inside of her, thrusting just as he did when he kissed her on the mouth.

The pleasure was sudden and intense, and she arched her hips up to press herself against his mouth. She clutched the grass in her fists to anchor herself to the earth as the climax took her. It was almost too much to stand. Her heart would burst if it continued. But when she tried to escape he held her hips in place and took her even higher before the last release which left her limp, wet and ready for his entry.

He pulled away and knelt to undo his

breeches. She rose as well, lunging to tackle him to the ground, climbing on to his body and pushing her skirts out of the way to take him inside her. Then she locked her feet behind his thighs and thrust hard and fast against him, moving on him with the same frenzy he had driven her to.

When she knew he was nearing the peak, she reached beneath the collar of his coat and dug her fingers into his shoulders before sealing his mouth with a musky kiss. She felt his climax in the shocked breath he gave and the sudden tensing of every muscle before he relaxed with a sigh.

She broke the kiss and relaxed as well, resting an elbow on the ground and her head on her fist. 'Does the club have a painting for that as well?'

He sighed, staring up at the sky with a beatific smile. 'If we do not, I shall paint one myself and hang it at tomorrow night's masquerade, in your honour.'

'We are going to London,' she said, smiling at the fun of fancy dress.

He gave her a surprised look. 'I have given you my opinion of your attending events at Vitium et Virtus.'

'But surely, now that we are intimate, it would be all right,' she said, running a coaxing finger down the front of his vest.

'I do not see how,' he said. 'The club is no place for a lady.'

'Yet I saw many women there,' she said. 'If you go without me, how am I to trust that there is nothing unsavoury occurring?'

'You should not even know of the place, much less wonder what I am doing there,' he replied.

She had meant it in jest, but his reply was hardly reassuring. 'But I will wonder,' she said. 'And others will wonder why you are alone, since we have been married less than a month.'

'No one will talk,' he said, as if this was the only thing that should concern her. 'I am the one who sees that no scandal ever escapes the place. The members are sworn to secrecy.'

'Not talking about a thing is not the same as not knowing it,' she said. She could already imagine the sidelong glances she would get when ladies of her acquaintance realised he had returned to town without her. 'I do not understand why you think my scandals shall be public and yours shall be private.'

'It was a rule you agreed to, when we married,' he said.

As she remembered it, she had agreed to nothing. She had told him specifically of her plan to break any and all rules when she chose. 'But that one makes no sense,' she said. 'And it hurts me when you go to that place without taking me along.' That was more truth than she'd planned to reveal.

Her honesty did not seem to affect him in the slightest. He rolled her off him and on to the soft grass that had been their bed. Then he gave her a quick peck upon the cheek before standing and doing up his breeches. 'I will be back on Thursday morning. The time will pass so quickly you will hardly know I'm gone.' Then he left her, walking in the direction of the stables, probably to prepare his horse for the ride to London. She could hear him whistling a few bars of the song she'd been trying unsuccessfully to teach the bird. It was some consolation to think that one of them had learned it. Would that Frederick was so easy to educate in the things that really mattered.

She rose and shook the grass from her skirts, calling for the dog before walking with him back to the house. By the time she arrived, she had a plan to teach her husband the benefits of shared entertainments.

He would not like it, of course. At least, not at first. If there was truly nothing to fear from Vitium et Virtus and her husband's continued fascination with it, then there was no reason she could not go as well. He would see her there and scold her. Most likely, he would become so angry that he would kiss her. Then they would go to the places there that other couples went when they wished to be alone, and he would forgive her everything.

But he would not just leave her behind, as Father had when he'd married Marietta. They belonged to each other now, just as the Bishop said at the wedding. They belonged together.

And if she should find that he only went to the club to escape her and to sample pleasures in private and fulfil desires that he did not wish to admit he had?

She did not want to think about it. She had seen him there twice. He had not been behaving any more improperly than he had when people could see him.

It was a shame, really. If one could not let down one's guard when all around them were doing so, what was the point of going to such a place? To cause him to make even a small misstep would be a service. If it was possible to commit a sin when one was with one's own wife. She was not sure.

She went into the house and up the stairs, with Sargent loping at her side, until she arrived at her bedroom where her maid was waiting. 'There is to be a ball at Vitium et Virtus and I need a costume.'

'Oh, no, ma'am.' Polly was still smarting from their last adventure and the risks she had taken.

George gave her a frustrated frown. 'Do not be so silly. I am going with my husband. If he owns the club, I will be perfectly safe there.'

'I suppose,' Polly said. 'But you do not mean to look like a fallen woman again, I hope.'

'I am not fallen,' George said with a proud smile. 'At least not in a way that society frowns upon. I am married now. And thus, I am allowed some latitude in my dress, am I not?'

Her maid had no argument against something that was so perfectly true.

George threw the doors of the wardrobe open wide. 'It should not be necessary to buy a costume, I think. Perhaps something old can be re-trimmed.' She pulled out a blue-green gown, the colour of the sea on a summer day. 'This one. Pull off the sleeves, cut the hem until it looks like seaweed. Take the pearls from another gown and scatter them across the bodice. And make me a mask as well.' She held it up against herself, swaying to admire the movement of the skirt. 'I shall let down my hair and be a mermaid.'

And she would not bother with the nonsense of attracting other men to dally with. In no time at all, she would catch the only man she cared for, lure him to the rooms upstairs she had heard about, and bind him so tightly to her that he would never leave her again.

Chapter Eighteen

His wife was a bad influence on him.

Fred smiled. Not a terrible influence, perhaps. But he was definitely different from the way he had been the last time he'd been to Vitium et Virtus. Tonight, he was enjoying himself.

The dance floor was packed with devils, angels, sheiks and harem girls, and any number of mythological figures in costumes chosen for their ease of removal. By midnight, there would be couples kissing in dark corners, embracing in alcoves, and leading each other up the stairs to the bedrooms. While it would be a lie to pretend that the whole world was in love, it most certainly seemed to be in lust.

For a change, he knew how it felt. He was simultaneously satisfied and wanting, content and restless. Once the music had slowed and the chatter of the crowd faded to intimate whispers, it would be safe to slip away, reclaim his horse, and ride home.

He grinned. His friends had been right. Georgiana Knight was the most amazing thing that had ever happened to him. He had not noticed how cold and unhappy he had become until she had come along to change him. Her scattershot manners were infuriating, of course. But try as he might, he could not stay angry with her for long.

He would be arriving close to dawn, when the first rays of sun shone through his lover's bed curtains, and he would waken her with a kiss. Her blue eyes would open wide with surprise, before putting her arms around his neck and dragging him back down into the pillows with her.

She had been angry at him today as well. But when he'd gone to say goodbye she had given him the sweetest of kisses and wished him a safe journey, their argument of the afternoon totally forgotten. She had not announced that she loved him as yet, but her actions spoke louder than words.

For his part, momentous declaration should probably be spoken with some ceremony and not tossed over his shoulder on his way out the door. He doubted he was capable of poetry. He had given her jewellery. And he had not just given her flowers, today he'd made love with her in them. When he closed his eyes, he could still smell crushed grass and buttercups.

There ought to be something more than just words to convey the depth of his feelings. As he crossed towards the office, he glanced around him at the swirling dancers and swayed along with them to the beat of the music. Perhaps that was what he needed. She liked to dance. He would hire musicians and they would spend the evening waltzing in each other's arms.

As they had in the past, masked women reached out their arms to him. And as he had done before, he disengaged himself and moved on. But tonight, he laughed along with them as he did so. While he was not precisely aroused by their advances, they did not leave him unmoved. Watching the abandon of the dancers made him even more eager for the night to be over, so that he might go home and work off the excess energy coursing through him.

Instead of simply walking away, he turned back to watch, just for a moment. And, as was true for everyone else in the room, his eyes were drawn to a woman in the centre of the crowd, dancing alone. Her gown was the green of a swell in the Mediterranean, the skirt tight through the hips and flaring out in a wave of ruffles and shredded ends, except in the places it was slit to reveal a bit of bare leg. Her bodice was a mass of pearls and spangles, giving the illusion that her breasts were bare under a spray of sea foam. It was accentuated by her long blonde hair, down except for a few small braids that held bits of coral and shell. Her face was hidden by a mask, covered with even more spangles, as smooth and bright as the scales on a fish.

Perhaps she had seen him stare, or perhaps she only sensed it. But she turned, looked at him with a tip of her head, and beckoned.

And, like any other wandering soul that came too near a siren, he went to her, his feet carrying him out on to the dance floor before his mind could register the risk. She was even more beautiful up close than she had been from a distance. Her movements were rhythmic, sensuous, and all too familiar.

Of course they were. He was not some innocent who could not spot seduction when it was within an arm's reach of him. Why was she alone? More importantly, why would she not leave him alone? She seemed to have eyes only for him. She'd paid not a bit of attention to the people around her, laughing and darting away from those that sought to catch her.

But to him, she held out one long, bare arm, beckoning.

One dance. Just one. He would discover her identity. And then, club be damned, he would go home to his wife. He reached her side and her arm snaked about his throat and she danced about him, bobbing and dipping in a sinuous imitation of a minuet.

He matched her step for step, wary, but fascinated. They moved well together, as familiar as old lovers. Had he been with her before? It was not Caroline this time, he was sure. She was as dark as this woman was fair.

But her identity should not matter to him. Without even knowing the depths of his weakness, Georgiana had absolved him of his mistake on this very dance floor. In turn, he had promised her that his attendance here would be no risk to their happiness. And yet, he was failing her at the first test of his loyalty.

Without another thought, he released her hand, bowed briefly, and turned to leave her.

Before he could escape, she was in front of him again, intoxicatingly close, her hand on his cheek, her body moving against his. His blood rushed in response to the familiarity of that touch. He knew her. He had loved her, he was sure.

He did love her.

As the song ended, he reached up and snatched the mask from her face, mortified by the truth.

'Surprise!' She could see by the shock on his face that, for a while at least, she had fooled him. A part of her wanted to be angry that he would be so quick to succumb to the charms of a strange woman. But since that strange woman had been her all along, it was hardly fair.

In truth, she'd watched him for nearly an hour and seen no sign that he had come to the place to bed another. He had been sociable but businesslike in his dealings with everyone else.

It was only when he had seen her that he had fallen. Proof that he was attracted to her, not because they were married, but because he found her desirable.

But now, he was staring at her as if he did not know her at all. The look he was giving her was every bit as cold as the ones he used to impale her with, when he had refused to acknowledge her. Then he grabbed her by the arm and walked towards the door of the private suite.

'You are making a scene,' she murmured through clenched teeth as he hauled her by the arm from the dance floor.

'I am making a scene? *I am making a scene?*'

'You are,' she repeated.

'You cavort like some Cyprian in front of everyone in the room. And when I put a stop to it, I am the problem.' He gave an amazed shake of his head.

'Cavorting?' She yanked free of his grasp. 'I was dancing, Frederick. *We* were dancing.'

'Dancing is only the beginning,' he reminded her. And that made him sound less like a sensible man than a Puritan.

'The beginning of what?' she said.

'You know precisely the sort of things that go on here. You questioned Westmoor about them at the ball.' Now he was looking at her with disgust, as though she had even understood what she'd been asking before he'd enlightened her to the ways of love.

'I meant nothing by it,' she insisted, offering a gentle touch to his sleeve.

Now it was his turn to jerk his arm away. 'That was what my brother's wife claimed, when I danced with her, here. And to think what might have happened, had I not seen behind the mask...'

'Caroline?' If he was hinting at what she thought, it explained so much. 'I am nothing like her.'

'You are becoming more like her every day,' he said roughly. 'It is why you are no longer allowed in London and why I do not allow you here. Perhaps my brother does not care that his wife is a whore. Perhaps my father does not mind that half the children are not his. But I will not condone such behaviour from my own wife.'

'I would never...' she said, unsure whether to be angry or hurt.

'You are right,' he said. 'You never will. Because you are going home.' Then he stalked to the bell pull to summon Ben to remove her.

'Alone?' she said, suddenly just as angry.

'I have business here,' he said.

'If that is what you wish to call staying away

for days at a time whenever you become angry with me.'

'I call it business because that is all it is. I have responsibilities here and cannot sit at home simply because you are too immature to be alone.'

'I did not ask you to stay home with me,' she said. 'Because I did not wish to do it myself. I came here to have fun and to be with my husband. And I do not understand why you, and your refined sense of propriety, are willing to come here yourself.'

'That is different,' he said. 'I am a man.'

She nodded in mock understanding. 'So. You wish me to stay home, by the fire, for the sake of your reputation.'

'For your reputation,' he contradicted.

She ignored him. 'And all the while you will be here, terrified of making another mistake.'

'I am not frightened,' he argued, just as he had the last time.

'You do not trust yourself. And you will never trust me,' she said, suddenly sure it was true. None of their arguments had been about her behaviour. They had been about his fears of things that would never happen. 'Tonight, I did nothing wrong,' she said, surprised that it was true. 'I was dancing. It was nothing more than harmless fun. But apparently, you are the sort of person who will not trust his own wife, even when she is in the same room with you.'

'The sort of person I am?' He stared at her in disbelief. 'I was honourable enough to marry you after I watched you behaving even worse than Caroline did, trying to throw away your reputation in this very club.'

'And thank you so much for your charity,' she replied bitterly. 'Perhaps I should be forced to pin a medal on you for such an upstanding moral sacrifice.' Their time in the country had been nothing more than a lie if he would not forgive or forget what had happened while they were in London. 'Since my presence in your life is such a continuing annoyance, perhaps I should remove myself from it.'

She regretted the words immediately. But it was not too late. Now, he would tell her not to be foolish. A single word of kindness and she could apologise. Then they would go home together and be happy again.

'Very good,' he said, yanking the bell pull again. 'Snyder will bring the carriage around shortly.'

She swallowed. 'That will not be necessary.

I will find my own way.' Hadn't that been her plan, from the first?

'Very good,' he said, making no effort to stop her as she left, unmasked, through the main rooms and out the front door.

Chapter Nineteen

She was gone.

He had spent the night alone in his room above the club, thinking it a fit punishment to let her wonder what he was doing and who he was with. It had never occurred to him that there would not be another argument, when he'd ridden back to Richmond in the morning.

She was probably sitting by the pond, watching minnows, but thinking of him. He would chastise, she would pout. They would reach some sort of temporary truce over this evening, where she would promise to be good and he would pretend to believe her. They would seal the agreement with lovemaking in his bed. Perhaps he would ask her to wear the mermaid dress that had caused him to make such a fool of himself at the ball.

In a week from now or less, she would do

something equally outrageous, or even more so. It was annoying that she was proving to be so difficult to discipline. But there was some small part of him that was looking forward to the conflict. He was not always happy with what she did, but at least he was not bored.

What he had not expected was to come home to Polly, the maid, packing the last of her trunks to send back to London.

'Where is she?' he demanded, looking out the window at the yard. It was a pointless exercise. The emptiness of the bedroom was proof that she'd vacated the house.

The maid did not answer the question he asked, proving where her loyalty was, he supposed. Instead, she handed him a neatly folded sheet of paper, closed with the GK seal that his wife still used.

The note she'd left had been succinct.

Frederick,
While there is much about the last month that I will always cherish, our recent pub-lic contretemps *is proof that we are sim-ply too different in character to continue as a couple.*

I know my behaviour shames you, but I cannot seem to last even a day with-

out breaking some rule or other. Should I ever manage to succeed in total obedience, I suspect your happiness will come at the expense of mine.

And it is clear, by your continued visits to Vitium et Virtus, that you have no interest in my feelings at all. Liberty is the reason for membership there. Were we to go together, intending to share its pleasures, I would not mind. If you insist on barring my admittance I must assume that you think me incapable of fidelity.

If you fear my disloyalty, there or anywhere else, you have no reason for it. I never wanted any man but you, nor did I wish to be unfaithful. I cannot understand why you will not give me the same trust as you expect me to extend to you.

After careful reflection, I have decided that to avoid further public embarrassment for you and pain for me it is best we return to the original plan of living separate lives.

If I require anything from you, I will contract your man of business to handle the matter, or relay the message. You may

*reach me the same way, or by leaving
word with Mrs Pimm.*
Georgiana

As she suggested, he consulted both the
housekeeper and his man of business to find
that her plans for the future were as carefully
arranged as they would have been had he set
out to take care of her. She had rented rooms
and arranged an economical budget for herself that would not deplete her allowance. She
had moved all clothing and personal possessions out of both his houses and was not planning a return.

There would be no need to communicate
over details and no awkward social meetings.
She had split the invitations they had received
into two different schedules so that they might
not accidentally run into each other at a rout or
ball. She had done everything in her power to
reduce the scandal of their parting and render it
as innocuous as he had described when they'd
first decided to marry. He could not have done
it better himself.

She had left his home without a trace. His
life would run just as efficiently as it had before she arrived, except for the bird, who was
still sitting in a brass cage in the library. And it

seemed even he did not approve of the change. Though she had managed to train him out of his exotic cursing, he now refused to whistle the snatches of song he'd learned in their place.

If Fred's days seemed suddenly joyless, he must remind himself that he had been satisfied with this life only a few weeks ago. He took to carrying her note around in his pocket so he might read it during those moments when his satisfaction wavered.

She had not begun by calling him dearest, nor had she ended by promising to be his always. He smiled weakly. She had never been the sort to couch interactions in false compliments. While some might have thought it rude, he could not fault her for a lack of clarity.

The note was what it was. It lacked the flowery sentiments of farewell letters he had received from lovers in the past. Their time together had been delightful. But such things did not last. It was foolish to pretend they could.

Marriage, however, was a permanent union. It was best to behave as adults in public and private, just as she suggested. If, when he read the words, he felt bitterly disappointed? Desperate? Ready to take up the pen and scribble a hurried apology, accompanied with jewellery and flowers. And to follow the lot with bended knee begging for another chance?

That was how romantic liaisons often ended. Not for him, of course. Not in a very long while. The last time he had felt so raw, he'd been at Oxford. His heart had still been young then, tender and largely untried. He'd thought the world was ending.

He must remember not to care. After a little time to grow used to her absence, he'd grow numb to the change. Lovesickness was easily cured with brandy, the company of fellows who had been similarly abused by the fair sex and, most of all, women. Lots of them. Pretty, fast, loose. The sort who were not precisely as heartless as men, but who could be paid to be sympathetic without forming foolish attachments on either side.

If she did not want him, there was no point in being faithful to her. And the idea that he had not trusted her was ludicrous. He had wanted to keep her out of the club so she might never grow as corrupt or jaded as his mother and Caroline. Let her assume the worst of him, if it kept her from seducing his friends the moment she grew bored.

If she meant to avoid him for the rest of their

lives, then Vitium et Virtus was the one place in London where he was guaranteed peace. She would not dare come there again, even masked. He would go there and behave as he used to, sampling all the pleasures the place had to offer.

After less than a day in Richmond, he instructed his valet to pack for a move back to London. The town house was smaller and therefore might not feel so empty. The city after the Season ended was relatively free of crowds. In the lethargy of high summer, invitations slowed and there were fewer people who might ask him what he had done to ruin what had become a surprisingly successful marriage.

When the carriage had been packed with clothes and servants he'd mounted his horse, choosing at the last minute to ride beside it and let the fresh air clear his head. As his valet, Biggs, came out of the house with the last portmanteau, Sargent pushed past him, racing to the carriage, getting under feet of the horses, and howling as if his life was about to end.

'Halt!'

Georgiana's efforts to spoil the beast had not ruined all his training, for the bloodhound stopped immediately, ran to his side, and looked up at him, waiting for the next command. But the expression on his drooping face was even more pitiful than usual.

He stared down at his friend. 'London is no place for a dog.'

The floppy jowls began to shake and a keening whine escaped.

'It might be different if you were a terrier, but you are too big to travel.'

Now, the whole dog was trembling as if he might collapse in a puddle of tears on the ground like an Italian diva.

'Show some dignity, man. And why am I speaking to a creature which cannot understand me?' Fred wiped his brow as if it were possible to clear the frustration in his mind with a swipe of his hand. 'Biggs! Put him in the carriage. And get the damn bird as well. Never mind common sense. Let us all go to London.'

The move did not help.

On the nights it was open he went to the club, just as he'd planned, ready to throw himself into the festivities with abandon. But though there were more than enough women to tempt him, in the end, he chose no one. He returned to the private suite, just as he always had, and drank far too much, though the spirits did not seem to affect him. It was almost with relief that he left as the club closed in the hour before dawn and returned to his rooms to fall into a fitful sleep.

The next morning proved that the brandy had been strong enough after all. His head seemed to throb with each movement. His body ached from clutching the pillow to him, as if he expected it to escape, just as Georgiana had done. When he went down to breakfast, he had no appetite for it. He felt the same at lunch and supper. Everything put before him seemed flavourless and unappealing.

He felt no better the next day, or the next. He spent far too much time at Vitium et Virtus, lurking there even on days that it was not open. When he bothered to go home, he sat in the library with a book open and unread, staring out of the window as if expecting a guest that would never come. It got so bad that Biggs all but forced him from the house, hoping that the sun would burn away some of the demons tormenting him.

Perhaps the valet was right. It felt marginally better to walk down Bond Street, especially now that the *ton* had moved on to more interesting places. And he could not fault the weather on this excellent late summer day. The sun was out, the sky was clear, and it was neither too hot nor too cold. He could feel his mood improving with each step.

It had been a mistake to hide inside, brooding on the past. But he had not been hiding, he corrected himself. More likely, he had been ill. A bit of distressing news, coupled with a mild ague had convinced him that his life was suddenly without meaning.

But that was behind him. Today, the smells from a nearby bakery were awakening a hunger he had not felt in days. It was even possible to appreciate the beauty of the women walking past, a thing he'd been incapable of only two days ago. There, just across the street, was a graceful armful, staring into a shop window at a display of painted fans. The sunlight made the blonde hair tucked up under her hat seem to shine like fine French silk.

Then, her head turned as if she'd felt his eyes upon her and she glanced across the street.

His stomach fell and his heart thumped hard against his ribs like a battle drum.

'Georgiana.' He'd said the name aloud, unable to control his tongue any more than he could the beating of his damn heart, which seemed to be speeding up, like some infernal machine springing back to life after a period of dormancy.

Never mind it, then. Let it beat. It was not as if she'd taken it with her when she'd gone. Nor should there be any harm in addressing her, if he saw her in public. They might be no longer be sharing a bed, but that did not mean they could not speak with civility when they saw each other on the street.

Or so he'd assumed. Apparently, their separation meant something quite different to her. If she saw him at all, it was impossible to tell. He'd sworn she had started in surprise as he'd called her name and glanced in his direction.

But that look lasted only a moment. Her eyes continued to roam, looking beyond him as if she had not seen him at all. A look of puzzlement had crossed her face, as if she had thought she'd heard her name, but decided she was mistaken. Then she looked directly at him with the unfocused gaze of someone searching empty air.

Once she had assured herself that there was

truly nothing of importance to see, she turned away again, raising her parasol and giving it an indifferent turn in her hands before signalling her maid to take up the packages and walk down the street, away from him and out of sight.

For a moment, he was stunned by the enormity of it, unable to move from the spot, as if her directionless glance had turned him to stone. She had delivered the cut direct: the subtle and most perfect insult that one gave when a person ceased to exist in one's world.

She had cut him, just as he had done to her when they'd first met. It had been a frivolous move on his part, a few months ago. He'd thought himself worldly and well mannered. He had wanted discipline in all things and all people. And he had been sublimely confident that the silly little girl would never become the very cog upon which his universe turned.

Now, his hubris was clear. She had turned the slight he had delivered back upon him, a thousandfold. He had opened his home, his arms, and his heart to her. And after a brief inspection, she had decided that she did not want to know him or see him, ever again.

It should not matter. He had been quite satisfied with his life before he'd met her. Now, he could return to it, just as he had intended. Everything was fine. He was fine. And he was not about to allow a foolish little girl to call him a coward around women and to rub his nose in his illogical fears of betrayal.

But if he was so sure of himself, then why had he nearly been overcome by the desire to run down the street after her, demanding that she acknowledge him? If she would listen, he could tell her that he had been a fool to doubt her.

He had resisted the urge, but just barely. No one had seen his weakness.

None but he and Sargent, perhaps. What had come over him to make him bring the dog? He had never given a thought that the dog might be lonely during his absence. But suddenly, he was sharing his house and his bed with the creature as if he owed it consolation for the loss of its mistress.

When he had returned home, the dog had been looking out the window, paws upon the glass in a most disobedient manner.

'Off.' At one time, he'd have had to give the command but once to have the dog respond. Today, Sargent would not listen. He continued to stare staring out into the street as if he'd assumed Georgiana would be returning with the master and must simply be dawdling in the road.

When he'd realised that was not the case, he had turned to look at Fred in a most accusing way, as if demanding an explanation for the loss of his friend.

'She is not coming back,' Fred had said, annoyed that once again he had been reduced to talking with an animal that could not possibly understand him. 'And you are my dog, not hers.'

This was answered with a low whine, as if begging him to reconsider.

'I cannot just apologise. She does not want me.'

The dog cocked his head to the side as if he could not quite understand this sudden change in affection. Then he wagged his tail, hopefully.

'I am sure you are right. She still likes you. In fact, she always liked you. You are a noble animal and loyal as well. There is nothing to dislike about you.'

The dog still did not seem reassured.

'She will be back to see you, I am sure.'

He crouched down and patted the dog on the head. 'But it is probably for the best that I not be here when that happens.'

Chapter Twenty

It had been three weeks since the night she left Frederick. That meant that she had been apart from him even longer than they'd been together. It made no sense that it still hurt as much as the day she'd written her letter of goodbye. It made even less sense that she was obsessing over a man who did not love her.

Rather, he'd treated her as a possession, or, worse yet, a pet. Dogs were not allowed in the house and wives were not allowed at Vitium et Virtus. Not that she really wanted to join his silly club, anyway.

Gambling was much the same anywhere one did it. Wine tasted the same no matter where one was when the bottle was opened. Perhaps the entertainment was wilder. But it was not as if she'd never seen a naked woman, since she owned a mirror. The artwork and statuary all seemed rather silly, once one got used to breasts carved into door handles and phalluses for coat hooks.

As for the sexual escapades offered? No matter what he thought, she did not want to be with anyone but her husband. Nor did she want him tempted to visit others, while using the excuse that he was under some obligation to be there as an owner. If that made her prudish, there was little she could do to change.

Little she could do other than to leave him alone, just as she'd planned. She'd spent a fitful night in the town house, then arisen early to arrange for rooms in Mayfair. Her belongings had been transferred without need of another awkward scene.

Things had been going well, until she'd seen him in the street while shopping. He had called to her. She had wanted to go to him, of course. Perhaps, after a time, she would be able to talk to him without feeling that rush of desire to go back to him and obey and behave, only to be crushed by his irrational disapproval. She'd had more than enough of that from Marietta. She did not need more from him. But for the moment, she was too weak to acknowledge him.

So she turned, pretending she had not seen him. Perhaps it was only wishful thinking that she had seen his look of shock out of the corner of her eye, as she had moved on. She did not intend to hurt him. But if it was necessary to do so that he might understand she was not returning, then so it must be.

'You have a visitor, ma'am.' Polly came into the sitting room, smiling more broadly than she had since moving to the rooms George had taken to begin her exile.

For a fleeting moment, she wondered if Frederick had come. Then she remembered that she would simply have to send him away if he did. 'Well?' she said, still waiting for the maid's explanation.

'Lord Grimsted.'

Father.

George stood so fast that the book she had been reading fell to the floor. 'Bring him to me, immediately.' As the maid went back to the hall, she smoothed her damp palms on the front of her skirt. Polly had not said visitors. That meant that she did not have to face Marietta again. But why had he come to her without any notice at all? Was it bad news, or simply a social call? It did not matter. It would still be a chance to see him alone.

Her mind eased somewhat when her father came into the room smiling. It was a tired smile, but all the same, he was not frowning as he so often had when she was still at home. 'Georgiana.' He held out his arms to her, offering an embrace.

'Father.' She came forward quickly, hugging him and kissing his cheek. The reason for the visit did not matter. She would have a few minutes' uninterrupted time with him, which was a gift more precious than gold. She pointed to the sofa she had just occupied and the tray of cakes on the table in front of it. 'Shall I ring for tea?'

He smiled and nodded, taking the seat she offered. Then he looked at her and sighed happily. 'It is so good to see you again, my dear.'

'And you,' she assured him.

'You have not visited us since your marriage.'

'I thought the object in my marrying was to remove me from the house,' she said and immediately wished she hadn't. There had been no spite intended in denying him.

'It was time that you married,' her father said, as gently as possible. 'I wished to see you happy. And it was clear that you were not happy where you were.'

'I was not happy because… Marietta and I do not get along.' She had nearly announced that she hated her stepmother. But the truth was hurtful and did not need to be spoken. 'I have not visited because we are not likely to get along any better, now that I am gone.'

Her father did not try to correct her. 'But your stepmother is not the only one in the house.'

'I wrote to you,' she said, swallowing the lump in her throat. 'Each morning. When you did not answer, I assumed...'

'So I have been told,' he said, with another sigh. 'But I did not receive the letters. When I did not hear from you, I thought perhaps you were happier without me.'

'No,' she said, unable to contain her sob. 'I missed you.'

'And I you, my dear.' He reached out and clasped her hand. 'I had hopes, when Mr Challenger offered for you, that you would be better off in your own home. He is a fine gentleman, despite what is often said about his family.' He glanced around at her apartment. 'It concerns me to find you here and not with your husband.'

'We have decided it was simpler to maintain separate households,' she said, wishing that she could sound more convincing.

'So he told me,' her father said.

'You have spoken to him?' She picked a biscuit from the tray and put it carefully on her plate, pulling nervously at the edges of it, until it was little more than a pile of crumbs.

'When he came to enquire as to why I had not answered your correspondence,' her father said, his look turning grim. 'I have reminded Marietta about the importance of my receiving all my mail and not just the parts she considers important. There will be no further problems.'

She had not been forgotten after all. But that was not the most important thing he'd said. 'Frederick came to you?'

'This morning,' he replied. 'He encouraged me to come to you. And reminded me that one does not know how vital a person's presence is to one's wellbeing, until they are gone.'

It was a curious thing for him to say. There was no reason that she should apply it to their relationship, since it had been directed to her father. And yet...

'That is very true,' she agreed. 'If you see him again, tell him that is very true.'

Chapter Twenty-One

It was another night at Vitium et Virtus and the crowd was overcome with the excess of their revels. And, as usual, everyone was having a better time than Fred. He stood at the back of the main room, admiring one of the latest additions to the entertainment staff, a Titian-haired singer that Oliver had brought back from Paris. The girl was a stunner, with an impressive bosom, all but tumbling out of her gown.

It was not her figure that fascinated him. It was the smile and the twinkle in her eye. She stopped between verses of the bawdy song she was singing to throw back her head and laugh as if she found the words as naughty as the audience did. He had never seen anyone so glad to be alive.

At least, he hadn't seen anyone so happy in over three weeks. How would he ever forget the past when everything about the girl on the stage seemed to remind him of Georgiana? His wife was nothing like the red-headed singer. She was shorter and with a body more boyish than buxom. She was blonde, not ginger. He had heard her sing and it was nowhere near as good as the woman on the stage. But when she laughed it was as if she had not a care in the world.

'Do you fancy her?' Snyder was standing behind him, looking not just intimidating but threatening.

Fred reached into his purse and tossed the man a gold coin. 'Give this to her, with my compliments on her abilities.' Then he found a second coin for Snyder. 'And bring a bottle of the good claret to the office for me. Then lock the door and see that no one bothers me, especially not her.'

His glass was empty and he could not seem to recall how it had happened. Fred reached across the table for the brandy bottle to refill it, to find that was empty as well.

Had he eaten? A better question would be, when had he eaten? It had been several days since he'd even bothered to go home, sitting in the private suite at night and sleeping alone during the day in a bedroom upstairs. He'd brought the bird with him for company, but it seemed to have forgotten anything Georgiana had taught it.

He could remember meals, but not the taste of them. And his body was sending mixed messages on the subject, as if trying to convince him that he was both empty and full at the same time.

'Are you all right?'

'Eh?' Clearly things were worse than he thought. By the look on Jake's face, he had been speaking for some time, but Fred had not even noticed he had entered the room.

'I said, are you well?' Jake spoke again, slightly louder this time, to drag him back to conversation.

'Of course I am.' His friend had no right to ask. By the shadow on Jake's cheek, he had forgotten to shave again.

'Then I suggest you begin to act in a manner that proves it. You spend far too much time at this club and you do not appear to enjoy any of it.'

'Physician, heal thyself,' he grumbled. 'You are here almost as often as I am.'

'Then, at least take the damn bird away,' he suggested.

'Damn bird! Damn bird!' the mynah cried.

'It reminds me of Georgiana,' Fred said, feeling like an idiot for admitting it.

'Then you have been away from her too long, Frederick,' Jake said, shaking his head.

'Frederick!' announced the bird.

Fred grabbed a cork from the table and tossed it in the bird's direction, making it flutter off its perch. 'I can't go to her. She no longer wants me.'

'Then make her want you again. Buy her a necklace. Say you're sorry. Tell her you love her.'

Had he ever done so?

It had not seemed urgent, when he'd had a lifetime in which to say the words. And then, she'd been gone.

'I love you,' the bird called.

'And that is no consolation at all,' he replied.

'I love you, Frederick.'

He turned, searching for something else to throw.

'Frederick. I love you. I love you, Frederick. Pretty bird, have a grape.'

When he'd taken it away from his sisters,

it could do nothing but curse. There was only one person who could have taught it the words it spoke now.

He lunged across the room and grabbed the bell pull to ring for Snyder. When he did not appear immediately, he grabbed the door and threw it open, shouting into the main room until the porter appeared at a run.

'Mr Challenger?' Snyder searched the room for the problem.

'Send someone to my house for fresh linen.' Fred rubbed his cheek. 'And find me a razor. Then have them bring the carriage around front.'

'I love you, Frederick!'

He smiled and blew a kiss towards the cage in the corner. 'And get that bird some grapes.'

Chapter Twenty-Two

If Frederick had been here to see her, he would have been impressed.

And if she was truly to live independent from him, she must stop thinking that, whenever she had a success. Progress was something that should be made and appreciated for itself, and not measured against the expectations of others.

But an invitation to a musicale at the home of the Dowager Duchess of Leddington was proof that, in the eyes of society, one had arrived.

George meant to use the opportunity for all it was worth. The gown she was wearing cost more than her last three ball gowns combined. The violets that trimmed the sleeves and the deep lace ruffle on the hem were as unusual for evening as they were for late summer, and each one had a real diamond at the centre, lending a sly sparkle to the skirt. They were a perfect match for the amethysts Fred had given her.

And there he was again, interfering with her placid thoughts. She took a deep drink of the champagne she was holding, trying to wash him away.

'You are so much better than I expected.' The hostess patted her hand condescendingly. 'The Challengers, you know.' She shook her head in disapproval.

'Thank you, Your Grace.' George tried to keep the question out of her voice. It was not truly a compliment when someone assumed that your entire family was incorrigible, but was surprised that one of you had proved passable after all.

But she was more than passable. She was perfect. Or trying to be. Truly she was. Her dress was immaculate and the height of fashion without being gaudy or immodest. As she moved about the room, her pace was sedate, her step confident. Her manners excellent. She did not speak overly loud or out of turn. She listened to gossip, but did not spread it. And she did not gaze out of the window when others spoke to her, as if she wished to be somewhere else.

On the occasions when she saw Marietta at a gathering, she spoke with at least the illusion of cordiality and did not allow herself to be goaded into argument. Even if she was out of sorts, she would not be the one to rip her skirt in a closed door and run away with her gown in tatters.

It was not precisely boring. None of the society events she went to had ever been. But neither was it fun. For all the dancing, food, and happy talk, there was a strained indifference about it, as if all around her were holding their spirits in check until they could leave.

And today, so did she. It really was a shame that Frederick was not here to see it. He would be proud of her. Not that she wanted to make him proud. She had but to maintain her dignity and make a favourable impression until it was possible to escape. This invitation would lead to others. And none of them would be issued by people who wished to see the latest scandal from the Challenger family: a bride who had abandoned her husband within weeks of the wedding.

But that did not mean the Dowager was not

curious. 'Where is Mr Challenger tonight, my dear?'

I have no idea.

If she truly meant to moderate her behaviour, she must remember that one did not speak the truth in public. Nor did one put one's true feelings, sadness, hurt, loss, out on display for the entertainment of the *ton*.

She smiled back at her hostess with bland indifference. 'Not with me, unfortunately. But he did not want me to miss this gathering, for he knew how much I would enjoy it. And I must admit, there are advantages to marriage that I had not foreseen. When one is husband-hunting it is all chaperones and propriety, living in dread that the slightest infraction could mean ruin. One never comprehends the freedom of going to a party alone and without fear of offending.'

'But it must be a shame to lose the interest of such a handsome man, so soon in one's marriage. It is barely two months, since the wedding, is it not?' The woman did everything but lick the cream from her whiskers.

The answer to her question was yes. It was devastating to suddenly be without a thing she had never known she'd wanted. But she would die before she admitted it. She reinforced her smile so that it stood as an impenetrable bulwark against nosy strangers. 'One evening is hardly a loss of affection.' She sighed theatrically. 'I do miss him when we are apart, of course. But I do not want him to feel constrained by my presence. I have been told that a man cannot be happy living under a woman's thumb.' The Dowager's husband had been notoriously henpecked—her comment raised a slight intake of disapproving breath. Since George had accompanied her words with the most naïve smile possible, the woman could not decide whether to take offence.

'Of course, my dear. But you must be careful. From what I understand, there are places men go when out of a woman's sight, that are not at all proper. I have been told there is a club on Jermyn Street and you cannot imagine the things that go on there.'

George could imagine it quite well, since she had seen it for herself. Perhaps, as she sat here, being the sort of wife that even a stickler like Major Challenger could be proud of, he was escorting a masked woman up the stairs to the little bedrooms on the first floor.

She took another sip of her wine and reminded herself that she did not care what he was doing.

Suddenly, a clanking and clattering arose from the music room that could hardly be called a melody. It sounded as if the poor pianoforte was being struck with a mallet. Slowly, the sound coalesced into something resembling a tune, accompanying a vocalist who was as enthusiastic as he was off-key.

The voice was most decidedly male.

O Georgie my dear, I would love you and wed you,
She laughed and replied: Then don't say
I misled you.
Sing fal the diddle-i-do,
Sing whack fal the diddle-i-day.

She was certain, the last time she'd heard the song, it had been about Sally. But now, unless the singer was serenading the Prince Regent, she had a horrible feeling that the words had been tailored to fit her.

'Excuse me.' She set the wine glass she had been holding on the nearest table and hurried to the music room to put a stop to the embarrassment from spreading to the gossip-eager hostess.

When she arrived in the room, it was just as she feared. Her husband was sitting at the pianoforte with the mynah bird perched on his shoulder like a pirate's parrot, pounding out a song in her honour.

She hurried to his side. 'Are you foxed?' she whispered, trying not to draw any more attention to them than they were already getting.

'Drunk in love,' he announced, turning to the crowd that was forming as if to embrace them in his open arms.

She sniffed the air. 'Your breath smells of brandy.'

'Because I needed to steel my nerve,' he whispered back, loudly enough for everyone in the room to hear. 'I am not very good at this.'

'Then why are you doing it?'

'Because I want the world to know how I feel about you.' He turned to the nearest people in the room. 'I ask you, was any man in London as lucky as me? And did any squander that luck so foolishly?'

The bird squawked and flapped its wings as if to agree.

'Shh,' she scolded, wishing she had a treat to keep him busy.

Then she turned back to her husband. 'You

were most sensible,' she whispered. 'You put me off to keep me from making a disgrace of myself. But you are being foolish now.'

'I did not put you off,' he said, looking almost hurt. 'You left me.'

'You said you wanted me to go.' For a moment, she had forgotten to moderate her voice. She lowered it. 'It was for the best. We have known from the first that we did not suit. And that we would be parting after the niceties were observed.'

'But not like this,' he said. 'Not in anger.'

'I am not angry with you.' It would be easier if she was. She would not feel so naked and exposed if she had anger to protect her.

'Georgiana!' the bird called, loud enough to draw people from the adjoining rooms.

'Please take him out of here,' she whispered to her husband.

But instead of removing the bird, Frederick reached into his pocket and produced a grape, tossing it to the mynah as a reward.

'Please,' she said. It did not matter how softly she talked. People were not just staring—they were filling the rows of chairs and watching them as if their argument were part of the performance.

'You should be angry,' he said. 'I berated you over nothing.'

'I disobeyed you,' she said.

'And you will do it again,' he agreed, smiling as though he was looking forward to it.

'I try,' she insisted, more to herself than to him. 'But I do not think it will be possible to please you.' She had been trying harder than ever to be good. But the scene they were making was proof that her propriety had been but a temporary success.

'Because I am judging you by the behaviour of women who are your inferiors,' he said. 'You have given me no reason to doubt. I have no right to control all aspects of your life.'

'Some men might say otherwise,' she countered. There was nothing particularly unusual about the notion that men had dominion over their wives. It was why she'd been in no rush to marry.

'Then I hope that they have found women who will please them,' he said. 'I have come to believe that, while some men might want a wife that bends to their every whim, total submission is not what makes me happy.'

She looked at him doubtfully. 'That is all well and good for you. But I must think about what will make me happy.'

'Georgiana!' the bird cried again, as if her objections outraged him. It earned him another grape.

Then Frederick gave her a hesitant smile. 'I suppose it is too much to hope that I am the key to your happiness?'

Had she ever seen him hesitate? To see him in doubt over her was both shocking and flattering. She relaxed into him, letting her shoulder brush against his in a way that would hardly be noticed by the other guests. She had no intention of making this mortifying interlude worse with an improper display of affection. 'Can we not discuss this at home, where it does not make a scandal?'

At this, he laughed. 'You do not want me to make a scandal? How far we have come, if you must tell me not to embarrass us.'

'Georgiana!'

Frederick was holding two grapes out to the bird now, not to quiet him, but to encourage him to speak.

George covered her face with her hands, overcome with embarrassment. 'It does not matter if we have come far or not,' she said in a whisper. 'We must stop immediately.'

'On one condition,' he said, ignoring her embarrassment.

'Anything,' she agreed. 'As long as we can go immediately after.'

'Where are we going?' he asked.

'Wherever you like,' she said.

'Propriety and obedience as well?' He reached out to lay a hand on her forehead. 'Have you taken ill? Perhaps you are feverish, for your cheeks have gone quite red.'

She pushed his hand away, horrified. The other married couples in the room were not behaving in this manner. Frederick, if he was sober and in full possession of his faculties would not have approved.

'I love you,' the bird said.

'Give him a grape,' she moaned.

'Not yet,' Frederick said, holding the treat higher so he was sure the bird could see.

'I love you, Georgiana! Love, you. Georgiana!'

'Clever fellow,' Frederick said, and tossed the grapes, one after the other, to the mynah.

'When did he learn to do that?' The last time she had felt so breathless, they had been lying in the grass together.

'Perhaps he taught himself,' Frederick said. 'Perhaps he misses you as much as I do.'

'I miss you, too,' she whispered.

'And do you love me, as I do you?'

'Yes. Oh, yes,' she said, smiling.

'Then let us go home,' he said, standing and offering her his hand. 'There is no telling what the bird is likely to say next.'

'He was trained by a soldier,' she agreed with a smile.

'Yes, he was,' Frederick said, pulling her close for a kiss.

* * * * *

*If you enjoyed this story, you won't want to
miss these other great reads
from Christine Merrill*

*THE TRUTH ABOUT LADY FALKIRK
A RING FROM A MARQUESS
THE SECRETS OF WISCOMBE CHASE
THE WEDDING GAME*

*And look out for
the next three titles in the quartet*
THE SOCIETY OF WICKED GENTLEMEN
coming soon!

MILLS & BOON®
HISTORICAL

AWAKEN THE ROMANCE OF THE PAST

MILLS & BOON®

EXCLUSIVE EXTRACT

Spy Bartholomew Dyer is forced to enlist the help of
Moira, Lady Rexford, who jilted him five years ago.
He's determined not to succumb to her charms *again*,
because Bart suspects it's not just their lives at risk—
it's their hearts…

Read on for a sneak preview of
COURTING DANGER WITH MR DYER

Bart longed to slide across the squabs and sit beside
Moira, to slip his hands around her waist and claim her
lips, but he remained where he was. If he could give
her all the things the far-off look in her eyes said she
wanted, he would, but he wasn't a man for marriage and
children. To take her into his arms would be to lead her
into a lie. Deception was too much a part of his life
already and he refused to deceive her. 'I'm sure you'll
find a man worthy of your heart.'

'I hope so, but sometimes it's difficult to imagine,
especially when I see all the other young ladies.' She
picked at the embroidery on her dress. 'I don't have
their daring, or their ability to flirt and make a spectacle
out of myself to catch a man's eye.'

'You may not make a spectacle of yourself, but you
certainly have their daring and a courage worthy of any
soldier on the battlefield.'

This brought a smile to her face, but it was one of
embarrassment. She tilted her head down and looked up

at him through her eyelashes, innocent and alluring all at the same time. 'Now I see why they only allow male judges on the bench. No female judge could withstand your flattery.'

'Perhaps, but a man is as easy to flatter as a woman, one just has to do it a little differently.'

She leaned forward, her green eyes sparkling with a wit he wished to see more of. 'And how does one flatter you, Bart?'

He leaned forward, resting his elbow on his thigh and bringing his face achingly close to hers. He could wipe the playful smirk off her lips with a kiss, taste again her sensual mouth and the heady excitement of desire he'd experienced with her five years ago. Except he was no longer young and thoughtless and neither was she. He'd experienced the consequences of forgetting himself with her once before. He had no desire to repeat the mistake again, no matter how tempting it might be. There was a great deal more at stake this time than his heart.

Don't miss
COURTING DANGER WITH MR DYER
By Georgie Lee

Available October 2017
www.millsandboon.co.uk

oin Britain's BIGGEST Romance Book Club

- **EXCLUSIVE offers** every month

- **FREE delivery direct** to your door

- **NEVER MISS a title**

- **EARN Bonus Book** points

Call Customer Services
0844 844 1358*

or visit
sandboon.co.uk/subscriptions